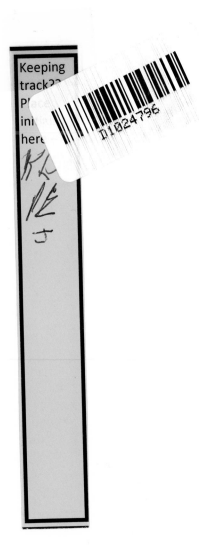

WINTER
MOON

Center Point
Large Print

Also by Lauran Paine and available from
Center Point Large Print:

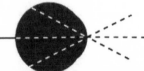

**This Large Print Book carries the
Seal of Approval of N.A.V.H.**

WINTER MOON

Lauran Paine

CENTER POINT LARGE PRINT
THORNDIKE, MAINE

This Circle ⓥ Western is published by
Center Point Large Print in the year 2018 in
co-operation with Golden West Literary Agency.

Copyright © 2018 by Lauran Paine, Jr.

First Edition
April 2018

Printed in the United States of America
on permanent paper.
Set in 16-point Times New Roman type.

ISBN: 978-1-68324-759-3

Library of Congress Cataloging-in-Publication Data

Names: Paine, Lauran, author.
Title: Winter moon : a Circle V western / Lauran Paine.
Description: First edition. | Thorndike, Maine :
    Center Point Large Print, 2018. | Series: Center Point Large Print
Identifiers: LCCN 2017059835 | ISBN 9781683247593
    (hardcover : alk. paper)
Subjects: LCSH: Large type books. | GSAFD: Western stories.
Classification: LCC PS3566.A34 W57 2018 | DDC 813/.54—dc23
LC record available at https://lccn.loc.gov/2017059835

CHAPTER ONE

Under the pale sky of early dawn, frozen turf ran on misty and silent and tufted-white with killing frost until it met the knife edge of a rising sun.

While he looked from the cabin window those first golden rays raced outward and downward and struck hard against the places where layered frost stood, exploding into hundreds of brilliant diamond-like facets of glittering light, some almost orange, some pigeon-blood red, and others blue-white.

He stood there beside the bed with his coat around his shoulders, his gun belted loosely around his middle, and his stocking feet pushed into mud-caked boots. Between the bottom of the coat and the tops of his boots, was the baggy ludicrousness of his long winter underwear.

He stood without moving, watching that eternal and stirring rebirth of another day, feeling in its beauty, its hush, its solemnity, the promise that life *was* eternal. Then he turned away, crossed back to the bed, and sank down there to run a hand through his hair and gaze at the papers spread out beside his bed on the floor.

He had consumption, and in the night when he was racked with coughs he had to have a place to expectorate. That's what the spread papers were for. On them were the little gobbets of blood.

There was a time when those harbingers of death made him frightened. Now, they only made him disgusted—and sad. Death came to everyone; a man died a little bit each day he was above ground; many men would die before Frank Reno died.

He got up again, went to the window, and leaned there looking out, but now his attention was gravely upon the little town off to his right and downcountry where the plain broadened and lengthened and ran on farther than a man could see. There, too, that fresh and new rising sun struck tin roofs and glass windows and little pools of frozen water, skidding off each with its dazzling brightness. There were two things in that town: a bank and an express office.

A noise distracted him. In a flash his smoky gaze shifted, went upland to the willow thicket which hid a corral, and grew very still there. The noise came again. He relaxed; a horse was cribbing—chewing wood. Making a grating sound. The willow thicket and the secret corral still held some tag ends of night, hazily dark and lingering. From that direction, too, came the tinkling of an icy creek.

He let his eyes resume their gentle appraisal of the new day, the land, the far-away hills. This was the best time of day. There were no people abroad to spoil it. No noise, no movement. Just stillness. Just that eternal promise to man that this day would be followed by other days. That life would go on and on. He'd often felt this, too, lying under a cloudless sky studying the heavens through a filigree of stiff-topped pines; there was in Nature a promise to man.

Someone cleared his throat in another part of the cabin, groaned, and turned upon a bunk with springs made of rope. Frank Reno turned to listen. The other man went silent again. For a little longer Frank stood by the window, then he moved away, out of his room and into the rickety kitchen. There, he wadded paper, pushed it into a greasy little woodstove, poked kindling in on top of it, and struck a match. Flame sprang out at him at once. He waited a considering moment, then pushed in more wood—all dry white-oak faggots because they gave off considerable heat but made no telltale smoke—then he closed the stove, set the damper, and returned silently to his room to fully clothe himself.

Afterward he went out for a bucket of water at the creek. While he was down among the willows, he forked hay to four sleek, racy-limbed fine animals in the corral. Then he returned to the cabin and washed. By then the cabin was warming up. Also by then, there was another man near the stove. He twisted to see as Frank came into the kitchen. This man was younger than Frank Reno and larger. He had on his trousers, but no boots or coat, and his gun belt was sagging heavily around his middle. He yawned and scratched his belly.

"Cold out," he said by way of greeting.

Frank nodded, saying nothing in return, set the bucket upon the stove, and turned his back upon the younger man. Next, he drew a skinning knife from the outside of his left boot, and went to work slicing side meat at a three-legged table someone had propped up with a box.

While the other man washed, making bear-like sounds as that cold water fully wakened him, Frank Reno slid slices of bacon into a little frying pan. Instantly, there arose a sizzling, and then in that cold and silent air the drifting aroma, warm and rich, of frying fat meat. Frank wiped his hands, put on the coffee pot, and stood pensively watching the bacon curl and brown.

His companion passed out of the kitchen briefly, returned fully attired, and went on out of the cabin. He was not gone long. When he returned, he swore and rubbed stiff fingers together.

"I had to be crazy to let Buck talk me into coming into the high country this late in the year," he said. "It's cold enough out there to freeze the ears off a brass monkey."

"As I recollect," stated Frank Reno, "it didn't take a lot of talking, Josh."

Big Josh Pendleton grunted and stopped

rubbing his hands. He put a hungry look upon the fry pan. "A feller's got to live," he said, "only sometimes I wonder if this isn't the hard way to keep alive."

Frank's head came up. He studied Josh a moment, then resumed his vigil over the bacon, saying: "You don't mean that. You wouldn't go back to riding for the big outfits if they begged you to."

Something flat and distant, and patently thoughtful in the way Frank had said that caught Josh Pendleton's attention. He put a steady gaze upon the small, older man. "Would you go back?" he asked.

But Frank made no reply. He simply flicked over the frying meat and raised and lowered his shoulders keeping his head down, his face averted.

"Buck'd like to know," said Josh, still watching Frank.

A third man entered the room. He had already washed at the creek and he was fully attired.

He said, looking from Frank to Josh: "Buck would like to know what?" He resembled Frank in a vague way, but he was taller.

Josh looked guilty and uneasy. He mumbled: "We were just talkin' about working for the big outfits, is all."

The lean man moved up beside the stove, shot Frank a look, and reached for the coffee pot. He did not smile but there were times when his tone was light and bantering, like now when he said to Frank: "Pshaw, you'd work a lot harder than you're workin' now and for a tenth of the pay. Josh, want some coffee?"

Josh reached for the outheld tin cup.

Frank forked the bacon onto tin plates. He neither looked at nor spoke to the lean young man.

Josh did. He said: "Buck, there's a look to the sky an' a smell of snow to the air."

Buck sipped coffee and puckered his face because it was scalding hot. He was looking at Frank again. "How do you feel?" he asked.

"Fine," stated Frank. "Eat your side meat."

Josh and Buck reached out for the dripping bacon curls.

A fourth man came into the kitchen and he too was blue-lipped and bright-eyed from washing at the creek. He was short, like Frank Reno, but with great sloping shoulders and massive legs. His barrel chest strained under the coat he wore and his jaw was thickly hewn and nearly square. He looked at the others and grunted something, then reached for a cup of that hot coffee.

"That damned creek water," he said, "is colder than a witch's kiss."

"You ever kiss a witch?" asked Buck Streeter, still using his bantering tone.

"Lots of times," growled the short and massive

man, whose name was Bud Given. "To my way of thinkin' it's the only kind o' female I ever did kiss."

Buck finished his coffee, put the cup aside, and walked out the kitchen door into the glittering new day. He stood still a short way off, looking downcountry toward that drowsing town. The others knew what he was doing—what he was thinking—but they said nothing at all. They just went on with what they were doing, each turning inward to his own secret thoughts.

Five days earlier and that many horses apiece, these four men had blown the safe of an express company at Burnt Timbers, Montana. They had shot up the town and had last been seen riding hell-bent for leather into the evening dusk, bound to the west.

But they had not traveled west very far. Buck had scouted the land and he had led them due south as straight as the crow flies, up and over two mountain ranges and down into the badlands of northern Wyoming, keeping always to the talus rock passes so that they could not be tracked down, and they had come to this abandoned shack in the late afternoon of the day before with Buck's promise that here, at the town of Brigham, they would strike it even richer than they had at Burnt Timbers.

The last horses they had stolen—roped out

of a big band running loose on some cowman's domain—were mounts as good as men could want. In each outlaw's saddle bag or bedroll was seven thousand crisp paper dollars from Burnt Timbers, and that was what Frank Reno had meant when he'd said Josh Pendleton wouldn't go back to riding for the big outfits if they came and begged him to. It was also what Buck Streeter had meant when he'd told Frank he'd have to work a lot harder than he'd worked this past year on the renegade run, and for a tenth of the pay, if he went back to riding for the cow outfits.

Frank ate the last of the bacon and pushed the coffee pot off its hot plate, tilting it a little so that it rested against the stovepipe. Behind him, Buck Given was at the table finishing up.

"Frank," he exclaimed, "you're a good enough camp cook, but, by golly, I'm sure lookin' forward to goin' down into that there town o' Brigham and loadin' up on some lemon pie and fried dark brown spuds!" Bud Given thought a moment then spoke around his final mouthful of food. "That's one trouble with this business . . . a feller never knows when he's going to eat next, or what it'll be."

Frank nodded. "Chicken one day," he murmured. "Feathers the next. You through, Josh?"

"Is there any more?"

"No."

"Then I expect I'm through."

"Your turn to clean up," stated Frank, and walked out of the kitchen to where Buck Streeter was standing a little way off viewing Brigham from calculating eyes. Without looking around, Buck said: "It looks all right, Frank. No telegraph poles leading into it and only two main roads leading out."

Frank gazed along the line of Streeter's vision and studied the town, also. Faint gray wood smoke rose up, down there, to curve away and hang along the base of their little rise. Some of it was floating farther back, toward the willows and up that yonder draw where the corral was.

East and west and south from Brigham that dimmed out wall of night was giving way to fresh daylight now, and this brilliance reached up immensely from the plain to the morning sky, dwarfing everything.

As Frank watched, the little town came to life. Men passed along the walkways, tiny-sized in that distance, but distinguishable, too, in that immaculate and magnifying high country, crisp pre-winter air. A ranch wagon bounced over roadway chuckholes on its leather thorough-brace springs and faintly, very faintly, came the ringing of a bell that Frank Reno thought must belong to a church.

He turned, looked upward where the mountains at their back bulked large and, in some hidden places, were still night hazed and dingy. Sunlight struck down into one of those places even as Frank watched, turning black stone tawny brown and dirty gray. Farther up where a snow field lay, the light flashed down at him, incredibly pink and lovely.

Buck's voice brought his attention back around.

"You and Josh were talking about quitting, Frank?"

An excitedly barking dog's racket came thinly up to them. It was a good sound. A homely sound. Frank listened to it, then he said: "No, just talking was all."

"How's your chest?"

"All right."

"I heard you last night," said Buck, still not looking around.

Frank said nothing. He always coughed at night. It was worse when he'd just made an exhausting long ride and that, he knew now, was what Buck was referring to.

"Frank, if you want to quit, just tell me so."

"When the time comes, I'll tell you, Buck."

Now Streeter turned, facing Frank head-on. His steely eyes were not especially sympathetic. They were thoughtful and appraising as though he was measuring a man as he would a horse, gauging the man to see just how much more he could extract from him before he fell or stopped or died.

"That seven thousand would set you up on a

little ranch somewhere, Frank. Or you could buy a hotel maybe, or a stage line."

Frank made a wry grimace. "Not a stage line," he said. "Never a stage line."

He nearly smiled, and this brought to the outlaw leader's voice its joking lightness although Streeter's expression never changed.

"I apologize," said Buck. "Not a stage line. But I'd never rob one you owned."

"If you didn't, I could name fifty others who would."

Streeter was briefly quiet, then he said quietly: "When, Frank?"

Reno shrugged. He put his brooding gaze upon the town again. "I'll let you know in plenty of time to pick up a replacement for me, Buck."

"You do that. Now we'd better get the others and ride down into Brigham one at a time and see what we can see."

They turned together and strolled back toward the cabin. Buck Streeter's whole attention was already turning away from the man at his side and closing down upon his projected raid upon the town of Brigham.

Up the far slopes the last night shades were gone now. The sun was standing well clear of even the highest peak and that yonder snow field was just exactly that. It no longer resembled a fairyland, as Frank turned just short of the kitchen door to put a last look upon it. The world was its customary self once more. Dawn's passing had removed everything that was a bar to man's ferocity. He could now soil another fresh offering for a full eight hours, or until evening came and the process was repeated.

"Hey," Buck Streeter called into the house, "let's ride! Josh, Bud, come on . . . we got work to do." He turned and headed for the corral. Frank Reno fell in behind him and paced along.

CHAPTER TWO

Burnt Timbers, Montana, lay twenty-eight miles from the bustling mining, timber, and cattle community of Sioux Pass. Burnt Timbers was in the heart of Montana's grass country. There was as much money in Burnt Timbers as in any other village half again its size in Montana. But there was no telegraph line and this was what occupied U.S. Marshal John Galloway as he sat in the Burnt Timbers marshal's office discussing the recent twenty-eight-thousand-dollar robbery of the Montana and Western Express and Forwarding Company office.

John Galloway was a graying man with a drooping longhorn mustache, green eyes the color of a wintertime snow field, and there was not an ounce of spare flesh on him anywhere. He was a professional manhunter and none excelled him. He was also a dead shot with either Winchester saddle gun or Colt six-shooter. He had a memory for outlaws that had only rarely been surpassed in lawmen, and he feared neither God nor man.

"If they went west," he was telling Burnt Timbers' town marshal, a harassed and grizzled man running much too fat in his late middle age, "then you can bet your bottom dollar they didn't go very far in that direction. What I want from you, Marshal, is some idea of the towns south and maybe west of here. The latter, just in case they're doing the unexpected."

"No towns west o' here," answered the town marshal, " 'ceptin' a squatter village or two, until you get danged near to Washington state. An' between here'n there is a heap of hostile Injuns. I think, if they kept on ridin' west, we got nothin' to worry about. Them Injuns'll kill 'em sure as night follows day."

"All right, that's fine. How about south from here?" asked John Galloway.

"Some mighty high mountains, Mister Galloway. But after that they'd come down into upper Wyoming, which is prairie country for a long ways south and then . . ."

"What about towns?" interrupted Galloway.

"There's some towns down there, o' course. There's Blue River an' Shoshoni an' Brigham an' Cutbank an' . . ."

"Do they have telegraph lines?"

Burnt Timbers' town marshal squirmed on his chair. He frowned hard over this question and rubbed the tip of his nose. Then he said in a drawling way: "No, they didn't have none the last time I was down that way. They're situated about like we are here in Burnt Timbers. Not big enough to attract the telegraph company and not so far from bigger towns that they put up much of a squawk over not havin' no telegraph."

U.S. Marshal Galloway stood up. He was dusted with travel stain and hadn't recently shaved, which made him look villainous. "And those descriptions you gave me," he now said, making a flat statement of it. "You're sure they are right in all the important details?"

"Plumb certain," said the town marshal, struggling to his feet. "I saw the four of 'em myself."

"All right," said Galloway, drawing gloves from his coat pocket and pushing his hands into them. "I think we'll get your robbers, but how much of the twenty-eight thousand dollars you'll get back is a guess."

"Do you know who those four men are, Marshal?"

Galloway finished with the gloves. He nodded without looking up and crossed to the office door. "I know who they are," he stated, with one fist curled around the latch. "One's got the lung fever and spits blood, another one's a big, brawling cowboy from Idaho, another one is strong as an ox, and the fourth one is named Buck Streeter. You ever heard of Buck Streeter?"

The town marshal didn't answer. Instead, he said in a fading tone: "You mean that was the Streeter gang?"

"Yep. Well, thanks for your help."

"Marshal? You ain't headin' back this time o' day are you? It'll turn off dark in another couple of hours and it'll be colder'n all get-out. That's a long ride, back to the railroad siding at Sioux Pass."

"Every day I hole up in some hotel room," said Galloway, "means your town'll get back just that much less money." He nodded and passed on out of the town marshal's office, crossed through a rising little knee-high wind to his saddled horse at the rack before the lawman's office, toed in, and swung up. He then turned and rode northward beyond Burnt Timbers with his chin tucked low in the face of wind coming off some snow field somewhere, and beyond Burnt Timbers cut due east and booted his beast over into a swinging lope. Twenty-eight miles was a long ride and that wind was steadily rising.

Six miles east of Burnt Timbers he topped out over a wind-scoured hill and saw warm lamplight glowing from a set of log buildings dead onward. He kept his sight upon that merrily twinkling light as night closed down over the range, and angled south a little to pass the ranch without drawing attention to himself.

In that log house, he knew, were people, perhaps eating supper or sitting by the fire, or just sitting easy, listening to the wind moan at the eaves with no idea that a vengeful horseman was passing in the night.

Fourteen miles out of Burnt Timbers with the

wind dwindling and the cold freezing earth and sky and air roundabout, Galloway rode more slowly, his face down behind his turned-up collar lined with sheep's wool and his gloved fingers stiff to the marrow, and steam from his breath hardening into little icicles that dragged at his drooping longhorn mustache.

He did not come upon any more buildings until he was within the trading radius of Sioux Pass. Then it was ranches again, stone dark now and faintly illumined under a pewter wintertime moon. His horse's shod hoofs struck down flintily upon the solid ground, and every once in a while he heard tree limbs pop with pistol-like explosions from the freezing.

Overhead, the sky was a curving great tapestry without any other shade than deepest black and the stars were so close he might have raised a hand to touch them in that deadly still and translucent air which knifed into a man's lungs causing quick shocks of pain from every indrawn breath.

Then he came at last down into the utterly still Sioux Pass, his animal's hoof falls the only sound in the tiny hours of another day, and rode directly to the railroad siding where a ramp led up from some loading corrals into a railroad boxcar. There, Galloway led his horse inside the car, flung off the saddle tack and kicked loose some fragrant timothy hay from a corner stack.

After that, instead of going down upon the unrolled blankets in the hay, Galloway stomped his feet, swung his arms, saw that the horse was comfortable, and left the boxcar, closed its door, and struck out for the Sioux Pass Hotel.

One man, awakened by Galloway's careless entry, peered upward from the corner of the room where the stove sat and rubbed his eyes.

"Howdy, Marshal," this man said, getting stiffly upright. "You must be nigh froze to death. It's five below zero. A hell of a night to be riding." The man broke off, looked down at his watch, and looked swiftly up again. "It's two o'clock in the morning," he gasped.

"Is it?" said Galloway. "What room did you put those trainmen in?"

"Seven. Upstairs and down the hallway."

Galloway stiffly climbed to the hotel's second floor, paced along until he found Room Seven, and kicked open the door.

"Get up!" he exclaimed ruthlessly to the men sleeping there, three in number and all mounded under blankets. "Rise up!"

Galloway's roar did its intended work. Three heads lifted simultaneously. Three sets of slackly puffy faces looked wordlessly at the tall, coated figure standing there in dripping gloom.

"Get dressed and get the damned steam up in that engine," ordered Galloway, his ruthlessness compounded by a lock-jawed look. "Move!"

One trainman said acidly: "Galloway, you ain't human. Bed down here until sunup, at least."

"I said move!"

One trainman pushed clear of the covers and sat on the bed's edge feeling for his pants. The second man also tumbled out. The third trainman still sat there propped upon one elbow. His sulphur gaze never wavered.

"Galloway," he began in a bristling tone, then he paused, blew outward a big breath, and swung his legs out until his feet touched the floor. "What's the use?" he concluded, evidently speaking to his dressing companions. "The man's made of ice inside and out."

"I'll be waiting in the car. When you're ready, never mind checking with me, just head south for Wyoming and keep your damned steam up because I want to be there no later than tomorrow afternoon."

"Impossible," exploded the garrulous train crewman. "We got mountains to get over, Galloway. Can't possibly put you down in Wyoming until maybe midnight tomorrow night." The trainman put a triumphant gaze upon Galloway. "Unless you can bully that engine into being scairt o' you and . . ."

But U.S. Marshal John Galloway was no longer in the room.

Sioux Pass had two cafés that stayed open all night. One was run by a handsome buxom woman with a look that said she knew how it was with men who were alone most of their days. It was into this café John Galloway stomped, bringing in an icy blast of air before he got the door closed. His gaze sought and found the handsome proprietress.

He said: "Lady, wrap something hot in a paper."

The woman gazed at him. "Like chili?" she asked. "That's all I have cooking right now. It's for dinner today."

Galloway didn't smile. "Meat," he said. "Meat and potatoes, and if they're cold it can't be helped. Make it fast. I'm in a hurry."

"Don't worry," the buxom woman said, turning away. "No posse in its right mind would be riding tonight. Sit down, stranger, and I'll fetch you some hot coffee."

"I'll stand," Galloway fired right back, "and I don't have time for the coffee, and I want that meat and potatoes wrapped up right now!"

The woman swung an angry glance at Galloway. Their eyes clashed, held briefly, then the woman moved smartly away, red from throat to forehead.

It wasn't long before Galloway got his packaged food and left the café, walking fast. He got back to the train and into the only car behind the engine and coal car, closed the door with difficulty, and at last sank down upon his blankets to eat.

Moments later the trainmen arrived, banged

upon Galloway's door, and hastened forward into the engine without getting, or waiting for, an answer to their banging.

Galloway ate methodically until the food was gone. He then removed his hat, tossed it down, and worked up a cigarette in brown paper which he smoked as the train at last began to move southward in a fitful series of starts and jerks. At each rough movement Galloway's drooping lip corners lifted a little more until, in his dark and secret place, he was smiling. This was the only way the crewmen of his specially chartered train could manifest displeasure and protest, and they were registering it. Galloway smoked on with the train picking up speed. Once, he looked ahead where his horse was eating, saw how all four of the animal's legs were braced, then he lay back upon the cushioning hay and killed the cigarette.

This, he told himself, had to be the showdown. He had trailed the Streeter band of outlaws from the Deschutes country of Oregon to Bend, to Yakima up in Washington state, then over to Boise in Idaho, and from there to Burnt Timbers, Montana.

Before that, he could chart their course from Texas westward and on up into the Northwest, always far behind when they struck, always arriving too late in some angry town where ire fell upon his own head.

But this was to be different. Galloway could

feel in his heart that this was to be different. The signs were many. For one thing, he would now be in the same country with Buck Streeter and his outlaws. With a little luck—and the smarting indignation of his special train crew—he would even be in the locality where the band was to raid *before* they struck, which would give him at long last an even break.

Another sign he considered now was that Frank Reno, the aging member of Streeter's outlaw band, would be unable to maintain the killing pace for long. Galloway knew of Frank's consumption. He knew a great deal about each of the men he was after. He'd had a hectic year to learn about these men, and memorize their faces from the Wanted posters. He knew, for instance, that burly Bud Given had a wife and baby son in Kansas. Bud's wife believed her man was making a stake trailing cattle north out of Texas. Perhaps, Galloway now thought in the musing gloom of his icy boxcar, that had initially been Bud Given's intention because he *had* made two drives up over the Canadian River with Dodge City beef. But that was before he'd shot and killed a gambler in San Antonio, and when the gambler had been laid out and his coat had been opened, he'd had no gun on him which made massive Bud Given a murderer.

Galloway also knew a strange tale concerning fast-draw Buck Streeter and Frank Reno, which not even Buck knew. They were brothers. Both had had the same mother. But Galloway had learned long ago that Frank had never told Buck this information. For what reason Frank had kept his secret, Galloway did not know—nor care. And yet, every now and then, this rose up to trouble his rest. The riddle of Frank Reno, who knew, and Buck Streeter, who did not know, was that although each had separate fathers, both had the same mother.

He thought now, careening down the frozen darkness toward Wyoming, that this had to be the reason Frank continued to ride with Buck even though he had long since been riding on courage alone.

Galloway had talked to a medical man seven months earlier in Texas who had treated Frank Reno. "He could probably live to be fifty-five or sixty," this doctor had told Galloway, "if he led a normal life, got plenty of sleep, good meals, and avoided hard exertion and dampness."

Galloway's slate-like eyes twinkled ironically now in recollection, for if that doctor had been trying to name the things that an outlaw such as Frank Reno had to exist without, he never could have designated them more accurately.

Frank probably hadn't had a square meal in a full year. Certainly, he had not been able to relax or get a full night's sleep. As for exertion and dampness, Galloway himself had trailed the

Streeter band through desert cloudbursts over endless miles when the fleeing men had abandoned one tired out horse after another until, reeling in their saddles, they'd collapsed behind tiers of sage to sleep round the clock before staggering upright to race onward again.

These were the signs of a nearing end that occupied Galloway on the night he was whisked south out of Montana into Wyoming on his blood-feud trail after the Streeter band, keeping him awake when all around him in the night, in the darkened towns he sped through and the hushed ranch buildings, people elsewhere slept.

Galloway's orders from the Denver U.S. marshal's office had been:

> Stay on their trail until you get close. Then wire Denver and at the same time alert all local lawmen to their whereabouts. Get posses organized. Run them to earth. That band is responsible for nearly two hundred thousand dollars' worth of robberies stretching over a one-year period. That record has never been equaled in the history of the West. You must get them, all together or one at a time, but you must absolutely stop them. Otherwise we can expect an outbreak of lawlessness which will be unprecedented. You *must* get them!

Galloway cleared his throat and spat. He sat forward to make another cigarette. He was irritated. *You must get them!* Well, dammit all, he too was worn down to nothing but hide and sinew. He was doing his level best. He lit up, rolled back a deep inhalation, and expelled it through chilled lips.

He would get them!

But beyond that—what? For a year now, he had thought no further than the next blown safe or plundered bank. He had, somewhere along this trail, lost something. He could not, right then, pick up the threads of his former life, although he tried. John Galloway, Texas-born and Texas-raised. A lawman since he was twenty years of age. Thirty-eight now and as gray as a man fifty-eight.

And tired.

Tired to the damned numb tips of his nerves and the topmost part of his skull and mind. The more a man did in the service of law enforcement, the more law enforcement expected him to do. It pushed a man up against every kind of odds, always piling them higher just to see if he could really emerge victorious each time. But there was always that one final straw, that one extra obstacle. Then a lawman died in a burst of muzzle blast and his soul went somewhere—wherever souls went—in a cloud of stinking dirty gunsmoke.

And *that,* Galloway now told himself as he punched out the second cigarette, could be what his meeting with the Streeter band could mean for him—that final straw.

He lay back, closed his eyes, and made himself sleep. Whatever the future held, there was no point facing it tired, if you didn't have to.

CHAPTER THREE

Brigham lay out upon the plain some short distance from the foothills. It was one of those old towns which had in earlier days been a trading post and before that a mountain man rendezvous, and before that an Indian campground for time out of mind. Its buildings ran east and west, evidently planned that way so that the backs of the buildings would break the wind's full force when it came in fall and winter to hurl its frigid blasts downward from those backdrop mountains, northerly.

It was a focal point of trade for the big cow outfits for miles around in all directions, and because of this, when other former trading posts had dwindled and died, the town of Brigham had actually grown as it had prospered. In fact, it was only a matter of time before it became a county seat.

Its main thoroughfare was called Front Street, which was the custom, and its crooked little side streets were either named after great men, like Grant or Washington or Hamilton or Franklin, or they had no names at all and were referred to locally as the streets where particular families lived.

Brigham had a bank called the Stockmans'

and Merchants' Savings Bank. It also had a branch line of the Overland Stage and Drayage Company. Both of these establishments did a thriving business. Then, next to the bank, which was directly across the road from the Overland Drayage Company's office, was the Brigham Hotel. Next to the hotel was Larson's harness works and next to Larson's, going east, stood Platt's Tonsorial Parlor—BATHS TWO-BITS, HAIRCUTS WITH BEARD TRIM, FIFTEEN CENTS. Next to Platt's, still walking east, was the Big Elk saloon, grandest, most popular, and most orderly saloon in Brigham. Of course, there were other saloons—five of them in fact—but they couldn't hold a candle to Dell Smith's Big Elk variety house. Next door to the Big Elk was a café and beyond it was the Brigham City Livery Stable. Across the road from the livery barn stood one of those partially remodeled old log buildings, a holdover from trading post days, which was the town marshal's office.

Brigham's town marshal was a droopy-lidded, slow-talking native Arizonan named Clem Houston. It was a standing joke in Brigham City that you could shoot off a cannon behind Clem Houston and he'd slowly turn to see what was going on—but if anyone made the smallest sound, like drawing a pistol out of leather or cocking a gun in the middle of a thunderstorm,

Clem would hear it and go into action like streak lightning.

Clem was sweet on Della Watson, the singer at Dell Smith's Big Elk saloon, and when he was not working or in his combination jailhouse-office, he would be at the Big Elk playing cards, loafing, or drinking a little. He was there when an unsmiling tall stranger packing an ivory-butted six-gun strolled in, fresh from old Platt's barber chair smelling elegantly of French toilet water, crossed to the bar, and had a glass of rye whiskey.

He was still there later, when two other strangers ambled in. One was a short and powerful man. He was picking his teeth as though he'd just eaten at one of the cafés. His companion was a big shock-headed man with a testy flash to his glance and a reckless smile down around his lips.

There was another stranger in the Big Elk that morning, too, but Clem hadn't seen this one enter. In fact, since strangers passing through were far from a novelty in Brigham, neither Town Marshal Clem Houston nor anyone else paid them any particular attention. This last of the four strangers was slouched into a chair at the stud poker table. His hat was on the back of his head, and, although he was broad-shouldered, he had a wasted look to him that matched the peculiar bluish tints of his eyelids. He did not appear to be a well or robust man, and yet his heavy rider's coat was carelessly tucked in above the exposed grip of a six-gun. But this could have been an accident. The coat could have hooked itself upward and inward that way as the stranger had eased down into the chair.

There was a goodly crowd in the Big Elk this day, and the corner stove, a huge, ugly cannon heater, was merrily crackling. It was cold out despite the fact that the sun was brightly shining. Men stood around talking or drinking or gaming, or just warming their backsides in front of the stove.

Black-eyed and scar-faced Dell Smith, owner of the Big Elk, stood beyond the curve of the bar sucking on an unlit cigar. He had been in the city of Brigham five years now and whatever he had once been—those were knife scars on his face— he was now a picture of comfortable prosperity.

As Clem passed him, Dell said quietly: "Must be a cattle drive passing through out on the range somewhere. More than the usual number of strangers in town today, seems like."

Clem halted and put his glance out over the room. It did not appear to him that there were more than the usual number of footloose riders around, but he said: "Maybe so."

Dell removed the cigar and surveyed its frayed end. "Della's in the card room," he murmured, then took out his Barlow knife, trimmed the chewed end of the cigar, and popped it back into his mouth. He watched Clem Houston move out for the back room. On his right stood a tall and expressionless man with an ivory-butted six-gun. He and the day barman were talking desultorily across the bar. Dell could easily hear their conversation. The tall stranger was saying something about guns.

"In Texas folks don't much cotton to hide-outs. They call Derringers black-leg guns. It goes hard with a feller if he pulls one of those little things down there."

The barman nodded, his attention only indifferently upon the tall stranger. "I reckon so," he opined. "A square man packs a man-size gun up here, too. Still, you'll run across folks carrying those little hide-outs every once in a while."

"Hereabouts?"

"No," answered the barman, swinging his indifferent attention down to where a burly man chewing on a toothpick and his taller, rumple-haired companion bellied up to the bar. "No, not much hereabouts. Damned few professional gamblers come here, and them as does don't usually hang around very long. Aside from professional gamblers and the like, you don't find men packing those little guns in Wyoming."

"Town marshals sometimes pack 'em," said the tall stranger.

"Not here. Did you see that big feller who just walked back into the card room? Well, that's our town marshal. His name's Clem Houston. He don't carry no hide-out, just that six-gun is all." The barman straightened back as the burly man down the bar beckoned to him. "Be back," he said, and moved off, leaving Buck Streeter with his elbows hooked upon the bar and his left leg raised up with its booted foot resting upon the brass pipe that ran along the floor.

Dell Smith tossed aside his cigar and, turning, entered an office, just off the bar's far curving. The bartender did not return. He was now engaged in idle conversation with the other two strangers. That older man with the tilted-back hat and exposed pistol was still gravely playing at the stud poker table. Other people in the saloon came and went, or talked together, sometimes laughing, sometimes swearing. There was the tinkle of glass upon glass, the soft click of falling chips, and a thickening haze of tobacco over by the stove.

Buck Streeter walked out of the saloon to stand a teetering moment upon the yonder boardwalk. A whipping little wind had risen and it was cold. He rummaged the town with an assessing gaze, seeing everything worth remembering, such as the location of the lawman's office in relation to the bank and express company office.

A drunk staggered out of Platt's barbershop, paused to draw himself up erectly and firmly fix the hat upon his head, then he struck out across the roadway looking to neither the right nor the left and striding along with the extreme care of a man wishing for others to think him quite sober.

A boy trailed by a raffish hound passed by and a handsome woman came out of a store across the way, threw a look outward, and found her glance caught and held by the steely eyes of a tall, lean man in front of the Big Elk saloon. She looked quickly away and moved out westerly. Streeter watched her for a while. The abundant fullness of her upper body sang across that parting distance to him, stirring something to life deep within him. When she was gone from sight, he went along to the livery barn and stood just inside the doorless opening to escape that icy wind. There, he made a cigarette and thoughtfully smoked it.

The bank was directly opposite the express office. That, he thought, was good. It certainly simplified things. From west to east was the bank, the hotel, the harness shop, a barbershop, the Big Elk saloon, then a little hole-in-the-wall restaurant, and finally the livery stable where he now stood fixing the sequence of these buildings in his mind.

On the opposite side of the roadway the only important buildings were the express office and, much farther along, the town marshal's jailhouse. In between were other stores, but they were unlikely to be important.

The town marshal did not carry a Derringer,

only his six-gun. Of course, when they struck Brigham, he might run out into the roadway with a rifle or riot-gun. Sometimes lawmen did this. Well, that was to be expected and they would be prepared for it. Hazards of their business, Buck Streeter told himself as he smoked and loafed and flicked his careful eyes back and forth.

An irrelevant thought came out of nowhere: *Damn, that had been a handsome woman.* He grimaced, dropped the cigarette, and ground it out underfoot. No time for women now. That would come later, after this raid.

They would have to rest for a while. For one thing, Frank didn't look good. He recalled that earlier discussion with Frank. It troubled him. He didn't want Reno to quit. There wasn't a better man anywhere than Frank Reno when it came to dynamiting safes and strongboxes. They'd rest, then, for a few months, after this raid. Frank could build up his health again and the others could do what they wished. For himself, Buck thought, there would be a handsome woman like that one he'd just seen, to pass the time with.

A swaying shadow snagged Streeter's attention. He raised his head. Frank Reno was coming toward him from the direction of the saloon. Frank had his blanket coat tightly buttoned against that icy wind and his hat was pulled down in front. He halted when he came around inside beside Streeter.

"Quiet town," he said.

"Bank's right across the way from the express office, too," responded the outlaw leader.

"I noticed that. What did you pick up?"

"The marshal don't carry a black-leg gun. What'd you find out?"

"The town's never been robbed."

"Is that all?"

"No. There's no guard at the bank, but the express company keeps a shotgun-man sitting around between stages. He checks in early and leaves on the next stage. It's an Overland Company policy. I've run into it before."

Streeter looked up and down the roadway briefly, then turned to pass deeper into the barn.

"Might as well head for the shack," he said. "Bud and Josh'll be along when they're finished here." He looked around. "How much did you lose at the poker tables?"

Frank Reno smiled. "Lost hell!" he exclaimed. "I won three dollars."

They got their animals from a hostler and rode out. Not side-by-side but some hundred and fifty feet apart, Streeter leading. Reno, poking along, had his face snuggled down behind the turned-up collar of his coat and did not see the little dog dart out to bark at his horse. He only felt his animal change lead and hike up one hind foot a little. There wasn't even any sensation to Frank when the shod hoof caught the little dog in the head, hurling him end over end for ten feet and leaving him crumpled in the dirt beside the south plank walk. Only when a boy's piercing moan of anguish came to him on that knife-edged wind did Frank look around and down. He saw the boy fall into the dirt beside the pup and knew instantly what had happened. He reined up, watched a moment, then swung out and down, and walked over, leading his mount.

He knelt, pushed the boy's arm aside, and ran exploring fingers over the little dog. A hot, large tear fell upon the back of his hand. Frank looked quickly up.

The lad was not making a sound. His jaw was tightly locked, but his body shook and his face was as white as snow. Swimming blue eyes met Frank's steady look.

"I'm sorry, son," he said. "Feel here. Right under my hand here. . . ." The boy did not move to obey. Frank withdrew his own hand and pursed his lips. "Tell you what," he said. "Fetch me some tape and I think I can fix his jaw. It's busted, but if you'll feed him soft stuff and watch over him, he'll make it all right." The boy still did not move. Frank rocked back on his haunches. There were several idlers standing by, looking down at him. He said a trifle sharply: "What're you going to do, boy . . . sit there blubbering, or fetch the tape?"

"Get the man some tape, Don," said an old man

from the boardwalk. "He said he was sorry and he'd patch him up, didn't he? Well, then . . . get along with you."

The boy got up stiffly. He made a wide swipe under his nose with a sleeve and trotted off.

Frank got up stiffly and considered the watching idlers. "Boy ought to train his dog not to run out at horses," he stated. "Lucky he wasn't killed."

The old man chuckled. "I don't figure he'll have to teach him after this, stranger," he said, twinkling a merry look at Frank. "Any pup worth his salt will have learnt his lesson right here."

The boy came dashing from the livery barn holding a spool of tape. Frank knelt again and went to work. He was not as inexperienced about bandages and broken bones as he might have been, and before the little dog revived, his jaw and head were adequately trussed up.

Again, Frank stood up, this time putting the little dog into the boy's arms. He stamped his feet to stimulate circulation. "Cold town you've got here," he murmured, making a little grin at the boy. "Now take your pup home and fix him a box under the stove and keep him quiet for a couple of weeks. Feed him mush and stuff like that."

The boy gave Frank a tremulous smile. He was no more than twelve years old and his eyes were the deepest blue Frank had ever seen.

"Mister," he said swiftly, with gratitude up like

a banner in his eyes. "I'm sure beholden to you. I sure thank you."

Frank drew his horse in and stepped up to settle over cold leather. "After he's well," he said downward, "if he runs out at another horse, you take a switch to him . . . you hear?"

"Yes, sir. Mister?"

"Yes?"

"I'll hold your horse any time you're in town."

Frank nodded. His expression was thoughtful. "Once I had a pup like that," he said. Then his tone firmed up and he reined away, saying: "But that was a long, long time ago."

CHAPTER FOUR

John Galloway's special train drew off on a sidetrack at the outskirts of Shoshoni and Galloway left his boxcar to stamp his feet and swing his arms and peer ahead at the town lights through the frosted gush of his own breath.

A train crewman stumped back to halt where Galloway was standing and say: "We made right good time getting here, Mister Galloway. Now what?"

"Do what you want," said the U.S. marshal. "Just be sure one of you is at the train at all times so's I can find the lot of you in a hurry if I have to."

"All right," agreed the trainman. Then he took a deep breath and asked the question which had been plaguing him for several days now. "Mister Galloway, just what the hell is this all about?"

"I'm after a special band of outlaws," stated Galloway, not once looking down at his companion in the frigid darkness. "The Denver federal marshal figures this is the best way to catch up to them."

"I see. Well, had they been up at Burnt Timbers?"

Galloway looked down now. "You heard about the robbery up there, didn't you?"

"Yes."

"They were there."

The trainman mulled this over in his mind for a moment, then turned as though to leave. John Galloway's voice struck him in the back.

"Mister, you keep your mouth closed. Don't you or your friends breathe a word of this to anyone in Shoshoni. You got that straight in your head?"

"Plumb straight," answered the trainman, and waited for Galloway to speak again, but he didn't, he simply moved off townward, brushing past the trainman as though he was part of the roundabout scenery.

It was slightly past ten o'clock. Shoshoni's night life noise was tapering off. As Galloway stepped up onto the north-south plank walk pacing along toward the center of town, four cursing cowboys loped past loudly lamenting the necessity of the long ride home.

Little squares of light shone in the churned roadway. Galloway passed through these places, moving steadily along toward the town marshal's office, alternately touched by orange lamp glow, then fading into full darkness.

He found the marshal's office without any difficulty and introduced himself to the sleepy man sitting there in a cocked-up chair. Shoshoni's lawman was named Al Hirt. He was a transplanted Texan with the courage of a lion and the shrewdness of a trap-wise old badger. He sized Galloway up at once and offered him a chair by the stove.

"Had some hot coffee," he said, "but it's all gone now. How can I serve you, Marshal?"

"Have four strangers ridden into your town in the past three or four days?"

"No," said Hirt, creasing his brow in thought. "Not that I recollect. What do they look like?"

Galloway described Buck Streeter, Frank Reno, Josh Pendleton, and Bud Given.

Town Marshal Hirt wagged his head. "Ain't seen any men like that," he said. "Why are they wanted?"

Galloway sighed. "Bank robbery among other things," he said. "Do you have a telegraph here?"

"Yep," replied Marshal Hirt. "They just finished setting it up last month. You want to send a telegram?"

Galloway did not reply to that. He drew forth some paper from an inner pocket, took out a pencil, and went to work. He rolled his brows inward and downward as he laboriously composed his message, then he sat back and read aloud what he had written, holding his head critically to one side.

U.S. Marshal Devers, Denver, Colorado. Have sound reason to believe Streeter band in area where I am sending this telegram from. It was them all right who hit Burnt Timbers, Montana. Will try to locate them here. Then will advise you and call upon local lawmen for assistance.

J. Galloway

Shoshoni's lawman brought his chair down off the wall with a crash. "Buck Streeter's gang?" he demanded.

Galloway carefully folded the paper in his hand, raised his steady eyes to Hirt's face, and said: "Send this for me from your telegraph office right away."

Hirt reached for the message. He scowled down at it. "I'll be damned," he muttered. "Streeter here in Shoshoni."

Galloway stood up. "Not here," he said. "Hereabouts." He crossed over to the door. Here, he halted to put a meaningful look at the paper in Hirt's fingers.

Shoshoni's lawman sprang up, correctly interpreting that look.

"I'll trot right over and send it off," he said. "Marshal Galloway . . . where do you think them Streeters are?"

Galloway shrugged. "Which way is the nearest town hereabouts that has no telegraph line to it?"

"That'd be Blue River," replied Al Hirt. "It's about twelve miles due west. On about another fifteen miles is Brigham. It don't have any telegraph to it, either."

"Thanks," Galloway said, and left the town marshal's office. He walked down the right to a livery barn and passed inside there to hire a horse. It was in his mind to save his own animal until he was certain he'd located the men he was seeking.

He rode out of Shoshoni when it was a little shy of eleven o'clock and covered the twelve miles to the village of Blue River in two hours. He might have made better time except that he did not know the country and there was very little moonlight to see by.

Blue River was aptly named. It sprawled for a half mile up and down a crooked riverbed which contained a body of water by that name. It was a settler town, which meant it looked poor and was poor, and where, in the cow communities, each hitch rack held saddle animals; in Blue River there were more teams at the racks than riding stock. There was another factor that Galloway observed and correctly evaluated a mile before he rode down Blue River's thoroughfare: where cow towns rarely retired for the night before midnight, if that early, a stranger could tell those settler villages by the way everyone went to bed about ten o'clock and even the saloons closed up for lack of customers.

Galloway left his hired beast at the livery

barn to be grained, then went along to the town marshal's office and banged with a gloved fist upon the barred door until, from within, he heard the muffled roar of an awakened and indignant occupant. When he was let inside, he stood silently waiting for Blue River's lawman to light a lamp and step into his boots and trousers. Then Galloway went through his sequence of questions again, after showing his credentials, and waited as unemotionally as always, for his answers.

Blue River's lawman was a converted dirt farmer. He was of average height with broad shoulders, corded arms, and blunt-fingered hands. His name was Plaga. Otto Plaga. He was not as impressed with the status of his nocturnal visitor as he was indignant at the manner in which Galloway had gotten him out of bed. He showed this indignation, too, when he gave Galloway his answers.

"No, I ain't seen no men like that, an' furthermore what's so important about 'em you got to roust me out o' bed in the middle o' the night?"

"They are the Buck Streeter band of outlaws," stated Galloway, and watched Otto Plaga's heavy and rumpled face smooth out at mention of Streeter's name.

"Here?" croaked Plaga, clutching his beltless trousers. "Here in Blue River?"

"I don't know that," said Galloway. "Somewhere in this part of the country, though."

"Why?" demanded Plaga. "What is there here to draw the Streeters? We don't even got a bank here, or an express office, or a . . ."

"I don't know why they're hereabouts," said Galloway irritably. "Hell, if I knew *why,* I could guess *where.* But you're positive no such men have passed through?"

"Positive!" exclaimed Plaga. He ran bent fingers through a mop of awry hair.

"Well, keep a sharp watch. And pass along the word that they're in the country. The more folks you tell, the better will my chances be of catching up to them."

"Alone?" said Plaga, eyes widening. "Four of them . . . and the *Streeters?*"

Galloway lifted his left hand and ran the back of it beneath his drooping mustache. "Not alone," he said. "If I find them, I'll call on you and anyone else hereabouts who is handy with a gun to help me run them to earth."

Plaga's eyes dropped away from Galloway's face. He clearly did not like the sound of this.

"Well," he ultimately said, his tone rising in a hopeful way, "this is a big country, Marshal. Maybe you won't find them. Maybe they kept on going or didn't even come here."

"They came over two mountain ranges on their way out of Montana," explained Galloway. "There were no towns between there and here. One of them is not a strong man, and he'll be pretty well used up by now. I think they'll be somewhere close by, Mister Plaga. I think they'll hit one of these little two-bit villages, too."

Plaga ran out both arms and held his hands widespread, palms up. His expression was doubtful. "The Streeter band goes after big stores of money. There is nothing like that in Blue River." Plaga let his arms drop. "In Shoshoni there's a bank. In Brigham there is a bank and express office both. But here . . ."

"How about a town called Cutbank?"

Plaga slowly and emphatically wagged his head. "Not Cutbank. It's like Blue River. No money, Marshal."

"Settler town?" asked Galloway, and the way he said it was not complimentary.

"A settler town, yes," replied Otto Plaga, and squinted his eyes a little. "You don't care for farmers, Marshal Galloway?"

For just a moment Galloway looked like he was going to answer that. He did, in fact, balance the idea of replying truthfully in his mind. But in the end, he said only: "I'm not here to make friends or enemies . . . only to find the Streeters."

Plaga inclined his head. He was glad Galloway had answered that way, for now that he thought about it, he did not know what he would have done had Galloway said no, that he didn't like dirt farmers, because, even in poor light late at night when a man was half asleep, the leashed ferocity

50

of John Galloway got through to a person at once. Obviously, U.S. Marshal Galloway was not one to argue with. Plaga hitched at his trousers. He looked back into the little steel cell where he had been sleeping. There were two bunks there, chained on either side of the wall.

"You can spend the rest of the night here," he said.

Galloway shook his head, declining this invitation. "Keep your eyes open," he said, lifting the drawbar and swinging the door inward so that a blast of icy wind struck Plaga, making him flinch. "If you see four men who might even be close in description to the Streeters, send word at once to the town marshal at Shoshoni. You understand?"

Plaga understood. He moved out of that cold wind's direct path and waited until Galloway had walked back out into the night, closing the door after himself, then he let his teeth chatter.

Galloway went along to the livery barn, got his horse, and rode back the way he had come. Once, just before he left the limits of Blue River, he swung for a backward look toward Plaga's jailhouse. The building was dark again.

Galloway made it back to Shoshoni in better time than he had used on the outward trip. He paid for the livery animal and went back to the town marshal's office again.

Here he found Hirt drinking hot coffee. He

accepted the mug of it Hirt poured for him, passed over to a bench along the wall, and sat down. There, he unbuttoned his coat, thumbed back his hat, and quietly drank the coffee.

"Find anything over at Blue River?" Hirt asked.

Galloway shook his head. "Only a clodhopper settlement."

Al Hirt smiled wryly. "No more cow towns until you get out a ways, over near the foothills. Brigham is the next cow town. The other places around here belong to sodbusters. They're mostly emigrants or foreigners or something like that. They got nothing Buck Streeter would want."

Galloway got up. He felt tired and wind-sore and drag-muscled. "Thanks for the coffee," he said, putting aside the cup. "I told Blue River's lawman to send you word if he notices anything out of the ordinary. All right?"

"Sure," said Hirt. "Be glad to help. Where are you staying, if I got to find you?"

"In a railroad boxcar on a siding just beyond town."

CHAPTER FIVE

Streeter had been through this experience so many times in the last year that he had each and every detail worked out to perfection in his mind. While the four of them were drinking coffee huddled around the stove at the abandoned cabin upon the plateau, he said: "What about the bank, Bud?"

Given gave his answer briskly, with his eyes upon Frank because it was Reno's job to dynamite the safes and strongboxes they raided. "It's one of those Cleveland safes. As you enter the bank, it sets far back against the wall in plain sight. It has that same painting of old Justin Morgan on it that safe at Burnt Timbers had, so I reckon it's the same model." Bud paused and shifted his gaze to Buck. "That bank does a real good business. I'd guess the safe ought to be chock-full of cash money."

Streeter nodded. He, too, looked at Frank Reno. "Take a look for yourself tomorrow," he said. "We've still got six dynamite sticks left from Burnt Timbers. They're in my saddlebags. If you think it'll take more, buy 'em in town an' fetch 'em back here with you when we meet tomorrow night."

Frank nodded and sipped his coffee.

"How about the express office?" Buck asked of Josh Pendleton.

"They have the shotgun guard who is slated to ride out on the next stage come to the office a couple of hours early and wait there. That way they always got an armed feller on duty in the office." Josh raised his shoulders and let them drop. "The old Overland Company trick," he concluded carelessly. Then he slowly smiled, saying slyly: "Seems to me they usually have a lot of money in the strongbox when they do that. Anyway, that's how it was in Oregon and Idaho."

"How many clerks in the office?" Streeter asked, putting aside his empty cup and reaching for his tobacco sack.

"Two," Josh promptly replied. "One sellin' tickets and the other's the bookkeeper."

"And in the bank?" Streeter asked, lighting up and putting his steely gaze upon Bud Given again.

"A manager at a desk," stated Given, "two tellers behind the grilles, and a feller at the ledgers over near the safe." Given, evidently guessing what each of them was thinking, now added: "But he's an old guy and I didn't see no sign of a gun anywhere around."

Buck leaned back looking from face to face. After a time, he asked another question, but now the sharpness was gone from his voice and he seemed satisfied. "Then that's how it is, boys. Any of you got questions to ask?"

Given looked up. "You going to scout the countryside tomorrow?" he asked.

Buck nodded. "Like always," he said. "I'll have the escape route plotted when I get back tomorrow evening. Anything else?"

Now Frank Reno spoke up. "I hit the bank," he said, making of it a statement, "and a pair of you fellers make a stand in the roadway. Who hits the express office?"

"Me," said Streeter, and stood up. "Anything else?"

"One more thing," murmured Frank. "That lawman . . ."

Streeter inhaled deeply and exhaled. "Like always," he told Frank, "Josh and Bud, here, will be with the horses in the roadway. They'll call him out, and put their guns on him when he walks out."

"I've got a feeling about this one," Frank said reflectively. "I've seen his kind before."

Streeter shrugged. "Then they kill him!" he exclaimed, and yawned behind one hand.

"Be better though, if this one could be brought off without shooting. We'd have a longer start before they come boiling out after us," Frank commented.

"That's up to the lawman. If he's smart, he

won't make a play. If he's not smart . . . they shoot him."

Frank sat without moving, his gaze fixed upon the empty tin cup in his hand. "One more question, Buck," he said quietly, without looking up.

"What is it? I'm tired, Frank, and I've got a lot of riding to do tomorrow."

"After Brigham . . . what?"

Streeter watched Reno's shadowed face a moment, then bent from the waist to drop his cigarette into the stove's glowing firebox. His answer came slowly. "I guess we'd better all take a long rest. Head down for California or over into Arizona and loaf for a few months." The steely eyes went to Reno's face and lingered there. "Does that sound all right, Frank?"

"It sounds fine."

"Then let's hit the hay," said Streeter, and started around the others, who remained comfortably by the little stove, and passed out into the cabin's darker rooms.

Josh Pendleton took up their empty cups and sluiced them out with water from a bucket. He lined them up for use in the morning and turned to cast a look downward at Given and Reno. "You fellers goin' to bed?" he asked.

Given answered: "I reckon. Only it's damned pleasant right . . . here." He grunted, straightening up on his chair. "I'll be glad to get out of this high country. Never could stand a lot of cold."

"Frank," said Josh, "how much you reckon we'll get this time?"

Reno shrugged. "Who knows? It's a prosperous town. Everybody seems busy and thrifty-like. But you can't ever tell. Sometimes a town can fool you."

"Maybe another seven thousand apiece?" persisted Josh.

"Maybe. Maybe nothing and maybe ten thousand apiece." Frank stood up and flexed his legs. "Maybe a bullet apiece, too," he said, and walked out of the kitchen.

Josh waited until he was gone, then spoke quietly to Bud Given. "He's not like he used to be. Seems kind of morbid."

"It's that lung fever," murmured Given. "It's been giving him hell ever since we got into this high country." Given paused to stare moodily into the red fire glow, where shifting light touched his features, making them old and unreal and somber. "Comin' over those damned mountains out of Burnt Timbers he must've spit up a quart of blood. I kept an eye on him. Didn't think he'd make it, and that's a fact, Josh."

Pendleton turned this over in his mind and came up with something he was not sure he ought to put into words. But he said it anyway, because he was not a prudent or even a genuinely loyal man. "What of that money in his saddlebags, if he kicks off?"

Given's head came up and around. Where pinkish light struck his profile, it limned the rock-set of his massive jaw. "As far as I'm concerned," he told Josh Pendleton, "if we have to bury Frank under some rocks somewhere, his money goes into the damned ground with him. And, Josh . . ."

"Yeah?"

"You'd better watch that mouth of yours. I'm here to tell you I've seen a lot better men than you are, killed for saying a lot less than you just said."

Pendleton straightened up. "What did I say?" he demanded. "I only asked a simple question. A reasonable question. What did I say to get you all fired up, anyway?"

Bud Given stood up, pushed back his chair, shot Pendleton a parting hard look, and passed on out of the kitchen without speaking another word.

Pendleton stood a moment longer listening to the footfalls of Given, then he muttered a scathing word under his breath, got his blankets from the cabin's parlor, and spread them out near the stove. He removed his hat and his boots, unbuckled his gun belt, drew forth the naked six-gun, and put it within six inches of his head, then lay down fully clothed, put his hands under his head, and watched the dying firelight writhe upward upon the leaky ceiling.

By Pendleton's closest estimate, Frank Reno, Bud Given, and Buck Streeter still had somewhere in the neighborhood of thirty-five thousand dollars in paper currency among their effects each, which was their share in each case, from the band's last half-dozen successful robberies. And that, Josh thought now, was an awful lot of money when you lumped it all together. A fortune, in fact, and if it was combined with the amount he also had in his saddlebags, it would be more than enough for a man to buy a good cow outfit, and still have plenty left over to stock the place with and operate on for a couple of years, which was as much as any man could ask for out of life.

As for Frank Reno, Josh felt in his heart that he could not last much longer. When he died, Josh meant to be there with the others hat in hand when Frank was buried, and if, as Bud had said, all that money went into the ground with Frank, it wouldn't stay there long because in Josh's mind that would be sheerest waste. They had all risked their lives to get that money, and damned if he could see letting it mold into dust in a lousy grave just because Bud Given was a fool.

As for the others, though, Josh was undecided. Buck Streeter was the deadliest gunman Josh had ever seen. Bud Given was fast, too. Josh knew he was no match for either of them. Still, you didn't have to stand up face to face with a man to kill him. There were dozens of other ways to accomplish that without personal peril.

And finally, a man risked his life in every one of these stinking little towns to get—maybe—a third as much as he could get in one fell swoop, this other way, and to top it off, no one would ever know or actually care about what happened to Buck Streeter and Bud Given. Or, for that matter, Frank Reno, if Frank took too long to die naturally.

The reflected firelight dwindled overhead. Josh watched it diminish. It was warm there on the floor.

Beyond, out in the night, the world was utterly still and soundless. That killing cold was stealthily descending. It brought a depth of silence a man could almost reach out and touch.

Then the coughing began.

Josh heeded this, gauging the wetness of it. It irritated him when Frank coughed at night. Not the noise, particularly, or the gasping which followed these bouts, but the knowledge that Frank's ailment was transmissible. That was what stirred Josh upon his blankets now. He knew very little about tuberculosis actually, but he *did* know it was contagious.

From another part of the old cabin Bud Given's voice came muffled to call forth: "Frank? You need anything? I got a little whiskey in my saddlebags."

The coughing was strangled off. There was a moment of silence, then: "No thanks, Bud. It'll go away directly."

It did. Frank did not cough again for nearly an hour. Josh was beginning to drift off. Then it came again, racking, convulsive, deep-down coughs which wrenched Josh wide awake in an instant. He lay there glaring hotly at those last little reflected flickers overhead, and under his breath he grated savagely, "Die, damn you, Frank. Die and get it over with!" He waited, but the coughing had stopped and that singing silence returned, deeper than ever. "Die and leave that wad of money behind. It'll never do you any good anyway . . . not where you're going."

The night ran on, hushed and steadily colder. Milky light filtered down over this range of the winter moon and all of the outlaws, excepting one, lay sprawled in death-like sleep. That one was Frank Reno. He sat on the edge of his cot quietly cursing those red-black splotches upon the papers at his feet.

He was weak all over. This was a feeling that never failed to follow up those bouts of coughing. Weak and sweating, he raised his head to peer outside where moonglow lay silvery upon the hushed world, and for some unfathomable reason he thought of the deep blue eyes damp from tears, shining up at him from beside the roadway down in Brigham. One of the bystanders had said the lad's name was Don.

Down the dimming path of memory Frank remembered another boy and another mongrel pup. Both were gone now. The pup was long dead and the boy, too, in a way, was dead. He was not in any way like the man sitting there in trembling weakness on the side of a broken bed in an outlaw's hide-out spitting out his life's claret. He was not like that man at all and yet the man had grown out of that boy.

Frank eased back upon the bed, careful not to start up another series of coughs. There was sweat on his face, his upper lip, and his pale forehead. By rolling his eyes the slightest bit, he could see the upward sky and its hundreds of stars glittering up there like flung-back tears frozen for all time in eternity. A mother's tears, perhaps, or a sweetheart's tears.

There was something in that still, gentle sky that caught at a man's mind; something that cradled him with its timeless promise. A man, he thought now, was born on this earth to endlessly struggle toward some obscure goal that was always unattainable, but always worth struggling toward. What was it—this goal? No man knew. No man would ever know.

It wasn't really important what a man did in

life. He could be a respectable man and depart, leaving behind a respectable memory. No one would really remember him. Or he could be an outlaw, lying fully clothed and armed, as wary as a lobo wolf, ready every moment to shoot or be shot. It didn't matter because, like the respectable man, he would not long survive in the memory of others, come that swift winking-out moment when he was no longer a human being at all.

What did matter, though, thought Frank, as he watched the purple curving of the heavens, was what a man did to himself while he yet lived. Others might forget him, but he could not forget himself. He could never forget the things he'd done which were shameful to him. Bad things. Things that harmed others and therefore irredeemably harmed him even more.

But a man could not judge his lifetime by any one incident. He had to judge it as an entire entity. Thinking back now, Frank's conscience was not altogether troublesome. He'd tried many things. He had not, like Streeter and Josh Pendleton, come eagerly to the renegade-run way of life. But he'd failed as a cowboy, as a freighter, and a stage driver. For a number of years now he'd been unable to hold any kind of a job. He tired too easily to match the endurance of other men, so here he was, living in the only way he could. But he'd not been an outlaw for long. Only a little over a year as a matter of fact. Therefore, he could judge his own lifetime candidly and quite honestly and not feel too much regret.

He was nearing the end of it, too. This was nothing he did not fully face and fully realize. In one way it disgusted him. He was still a young man in his thirties. Much too young yet to die. In another way it saddened him. He'd had all the shining dreams men shared, and now he knew that all those wonderful notions were never going to come to pass for him.

Who should be blamed for this? God? No. Actually, there was no one at fault. A man was born, he lived, and he died. Life was a gift. It was a kind of promise to man that it never really ended. Therefore, actually, one man's life was not important. He should not hate so to part with it.

Maybe, thought Frank Reno, nearing the end of his life, if he'd had a wife, a son like the boy with the pup down in Brigham, he would hate to leave. But he had none of those things, never had had them, so the leave-taking would be for him only a quiet moment of sad regret.

He closed his eyes to sleep. Beyond, in the night, a little lost wind touched down for a second upon the cabin roof, then fled away.

Chapter Six

In Marshal Hirt's office, John Galloway sucked at his teeth. He'd just finished the first decent meal he'd had in two weeks—flapjacks with maple syrup washed down with a quart of black coffee. He'd shaved, too, and this was a great improvement. In fact, until one looked into his eyes, one might have thought Galloway was a rancher or perhaps a liveryman. Only his flashing glance said differently.

He watched Hirt's powerful effort at making a rough map of the countryside, eyes narrowed and brows down in strong concentration. Then Hirt finished the map and leaned far back at his desk to view his handiwork.

"That's it," he said to Galloway. "It'll be off a few miles one way or the other, but that's about how the land lies."

"Brigham is the place I'm interested in," murmured Galloway. "I ruled Shoshoni out when you told me there was a telegraph line there."

At mention of the word telegraph, Al Hirt started, lunged across his desk, caught up an envelope, and swiftly pushed it out at Galloway.

"Forgot," he mumbled. "This came in for you early this morning."

Galloway took the note, opened it, read it

without changing expression, and pocketed it.

Hirt, waiting, showed disappointment, but he said nothing, and reverted to critically considering his map.

"I guess you ruled out Blue River, too," he said.

"Yeah. And Cutbank as well. Squatter towns wouldn't interest Buck Streeter any more than they'd interest me . . . was I in his line of work."

"That leaves just Brigham then," agreed Hirt, taking up the paper and passing it over to Galloway. Then he said: "But what if they aren't around Brigham . . . then what'll you do?"

Galloway was frowning over the map when he answered. "Keep looking. Just keep right on hunting them. I don't expect this to end easy, Mister Hirt. Manhunting isn't an easy trade any time." Galloway bent over to trace out some wriggled lines on Hirt's map. "What are these things . . . hills?"

"Sort of. Foothills where your finger is, but farther back, north and west of Brigham, they're pretty big mountains."

Galloway drew back. He very meticulously folded the map and put it into a shirt pocket. "One thing I've noticed about the Streeter gang. They never get caught out on the plains. They always got mountains close by. I reckon Buck thinks like an Indian. In a bad spot, if you got hills around you, you got protection."

As Galloway stood up, he drew forth a pair

of new gloves from his blanket coat and began pulling them on.

Town Marshal Al Hirt said: "You get to know outlaws pretty well when you've been on their trail for as long as you've been following this bunch."

Galloway looked over and nodded. He was thinking of Frank Reno's secret when he said: "You'd be surprised how much I know about the Streeters." He crossed to the door, nodded once, and passed out of the office.

Behind, alone in his jailhouse, Al Hirt pursed his lips, wagged his head ruefully, and told a fly-specked lithograph of Abraham Lincoln: "You can be glad that feller isn't on your trail, Mister Lincoln. I've seen my share of cold-blooded men, but that feller takes the blue ribbon in my book."

Galloway had his own horse tied at Al Hirt's horse rack. He mounted him and wheeled away to cut out of Shoshoni westbound. He had a Winchester in the boot under his right *rosadero*, the wide leather shield attached to the back of his leather on his stirrup, and beneath the blanket coat was a recently filled shell belt and tied-down six-gun. Also beneath the coat and pinned upon his shirtfront for the first time in a week, was his little nickel star set within its shiny circlet, with the words **U.S. Marshal** stamped across it.

John Galloway was anticipating war and he was prepared for it.

As he rode through a raw new day little shafts of dagger-like sunshine came down from an overcast sky. The air had a faintly metallic scent to it, which meant snow in the high country, and the air itself was cold enough to make a man's steaming breath congeal upon his whiskers.

Galloway was an experienced man at this thing he was now doing. As he passed over the country east of Blue River he noted the distance between trees, the little lifts and rises that intersected his passage west, and all those details which to others might have been nothing but the parts of a countryside, but which were to hunted men and those who hunted them, sometimes the difference between life and death, after the chase began.

When Blue River hove to hull-down upon the graying horizon, Galloway reined off northward a little ways so that he could bypass the place. In his eyes, Blue River was ugly and the people who sustained it were from a different world than the one which had formed him, and which had sustained him, too. John Galloway had begun life on a cow ranch, and he had matured in that environment. He did not now, and never had, liked the company of homesteaders. There was only one other set of people he liked as little as sodbusters, and those other people were sheepmen.

The country on west from Blue River was new to him. Here, he made no effort at haste. Here, too, he studied the land's peculiarities—its arroyos and its every lift and drop.

Near noon he drew down at a freshwater creek with a hard rind of ice on either bank, and offered his horse water. The animal did not drink, but he evidenced interest in some willows, so Galloway loosened the *cincha* and let him trail his reins as he nibbled at those nearly frozen stalks.

Far off and not too clear now, with that snowstorm's deepening gloom darkening the world, stood a series of stark mountains, one behind the other, which bulked large upon the horizon. Galloway stroked his longhorn mustache as he stood there gazing upon these upthrusts. He was working it out in his mind how these mountains stood in relation to the Streeter band's race southward out of Montana.

While he waited for his animal to get its noonday bait, he oriented himself, and, later, when he crossed over to tug up the *cincha*, turn the horse, and step across him, Galloway had an accurate etching in his mind of the entire country between Burnt Timbers and Brigham, northward.

As he pushed along steadily, ignoring that increasing murkiness which promised snow unless a hard wind came to break up the storm or send it elsewhere, Galloway turned his full attention upon the country south and west of Brigham. The town itself was not yet in view, but he knew from Marshal Hirt's map it had to be dead ahead.

Southward lay the smooth flow of Wyoming's great plains. Visibility here was limited for Galloway but he was no stranger in a general way to these miles and miles of Wyoming prairie, and he was satisfied, from what he'd gleaned of Buck Streeter after a year-long hunt, that the outlaws would not seek escape down that endless range where no cover existed.

He eliminated those sharp-standing mountains, too. Streeter would not risk returning to southern Montana. Not now, after what he'd done at Burnt Timbers. There was another reason, also, why he'd never risk the northward route again. This oncoming storm would dump thirty feet of snow in the upland passes. No man alive, and no horse, would be able to get through once the storm broke.

That left the eastern and western escape routes. Galloway hoped Streeter would flee east. If he did that, the clodhoppers at Blue River would be baying at his heels as well as that sharp-eyed and forewarned town marshal back at Shoshoni.

There was only the western route left open then, and Galloway removed one glove, fished out that telegram he'd received from the U.S. marshal down at Denver, and re-read it.

Am sending eleven more deputies to aid you. Have instructed one to await you at Shoshoni. Have ordered the others to alert the large cow outfits and towns west and south of Brigham, Cutbank, and Blue River. To form armed posses and await your instructions. Remember, the Streeter band must not get away this time. Will come north myself if you so advise me.

Devers,
Denver

He tucked the telegram back into his shirt pocket, rebuttoned his coat, and thoughtfully tugged the glove back over his gun hand. There was one chance in a hundred Buck Streeter could lead his outlaws through this surround, but only one chance, and Galloway himself was riding now to eliminate that, if he could.

His horse picked up its gait a little. Galloway glanced at its ears, saw how they were pointed onward, and peered ahead. A few little ragged stabs of orange lamplight showed far out. Too many to be a ranch and too few to be much of a town. Still, he was yet a long way off and as he rode along, other little lights appeared, rounding out the full complement of lamps which showed how the town of Brigham lay, not north and south as Shoshoni and Blue River lay, but east and west with the town's northern environs holding their backs to the mountains.

Something either developed in a manhunter or built into him at birth, rose up now to flash out along Galloway's nerves with a warning. It affected him in many ways, this strange premonition. It made the air smell sharper to him; it increased the range of vision and gave depth, sharpness, to his sight. It also stirred within him an age-old primitive eagerness, a quickening thrill to the imminence of peril and combat. It was the sixth sense that warned fighting men and manhunters since the dawn of life, that an end to their quest was near. Galloway recognized it instantly for what it was, and he was no stranger to this inexplicable phenomenon at all. He never questioned it, he only abided by it, as now, by drawing up straighter in the saddle, by loosening the bottom buttons of his coat where his gun belt lay, and by closing all his attention down upon that looming cow town dead ahead.

He did not fear recognition by the outlaws. He did not believe they had any idea a solitary lawman had been on their trail these past many months. What he did fear was some inadvertent thing spoiling his plans or his aim. It was not unknown for outlaws needing rest to buy off a town marshal or a county sheriff, or even, but not so often, a federal U.S. marshal.

He came down upon Brigham from the east and did not scout the town at all. For one reason he was confident anyone who saw him riding in would pay him no heed. For another reason the weather had turned intensely cold the last few miles, and now, upon the outskirts of Brigham, a few fat, lazy snowflakes floated down to gently settle upon his animal's neck. They were, he knew from the size of them, a prelude of what was to come. He did not mean to get caught out on the plain somewhere when the storm hit. A rider in strange country in a blinding snowstorm could ride in a circle within a half mile of a village and never find it.

Brigham's stores were lighted and people passed along the plank walks on both sides of the roadway. It seemed to be evening, but actually it was only three o'clock in the afternoon when Galloway reined into the livery barn and got down stiffly, looking back out where those lazy, big flakes were falling with increasing force now.

"Goin' to be a real pee-dinger," said the hostler who came forth to take Galloway's mount. "You made it just in time, stranger."

Galloway nodded, saying nothing about the storm. He removed a glove, dug for some coins, and passed them across to the hostler.

"Grain him and rub him down good," he ordered. "Then put him in a stall and fill the manger with the best hay you've got."

"I'll do it," said the hostler, squinting at the coins. "He'll get good care here, mister."

Galloway walked away. He stopped once on the yonder plank walk and drifted a narrowed glance westerly toward Clem Houston's jailhouse. He was thoughtful now, and full of extreme caution. Finally, deciding to size up Brigham's lawman before approaching him—in case he'd been bought off—he struck out across the roadway toward a little café with cheerfully frosted windows.

He stopped once before entering the café and looked around, saw the hotel, the Big Elk saloon, the harness shop, and Platt's Tonsorial Parlor, then pushed on inside that little café where warmth and rich aroma simultaneously struck him.

CHAPTER SEVEN

Buck Streeter left the hide-out at dawn. Frank Reno, Bud Given, and Josh Pendleton arose sometime later, ate a leisurely breakfast, and stayed for a time near the kitchen stove.

"This dog-goned country," stated Bud, "gets colder every day."

"Well," explained Josh matter-of-factly, "winter's coming. What did you expect?"

"It's not what I expect that matters," grumbled Given. "It's simply that I'd give a good horse to be back in south Texas right now."

"And leave the money in Brigham?" queried Josh, as he washed their tin cups and cooking ware.

Bud had no immediate answer to that.

Frank went outside. He did not return for some little time, and, when he did, he was blowing on his hands. "I wouldn't want to be in Buck's boots today," he told the other two outlaws. "There's a snowstorm comin' or I'm a Dutchman's uncle. You can smell it in the air and that northern sky is darkening."

"That," exclaimed Given dourly, "will be just fine! Nothing we need more right now than a damned snowstorm." He turned to put a steady gaze upon Frank. "I think we waited too long. We can't hit the town and hope to get away if there's a couple o' feet o' snow on the ground."

Frank was unperturbed. "Let's worry after Buck gets back. He'll have some ideas. Meantime, let's head down off this ice-house damned hill and get next to that stove in the Big Elk."

Josh and Bud were instantly agreeable, and as they left the shack bound for the corral, Bud said plaintively: "Let's stay down there. If we come back here, we got to chop firewood and that's not easy without an axe."

They rigged-out up the cañon where that secret corral was, got astride, and went stiffly jogging downhill toward Brigham. Frank sat on his right hand and held his reins in the left. He critically studied that fish-belly sky and shortly before they came upon the eastern end of town, he told the others the storm would probably hit about three o'clock that same afternoon.

Bud growled something indistinguishable from down behind the turned-up collar of his coat.

Josh Pendleton chuckled at this, saying to Frank: "I never saw a feller that hates snow and cold as bad as Bud does."

They were passing along before a number of shacks at Brigham's easternmost extremity and the ground underfoot was bleak and brittle so that their horses' hoof falls made a loud ringing.

Frank was slightly ahead when the boy ran out into the roadway, a tasseled hat upon his head drawn low over both ears and a grin as big as all outdoors splitting his features.

"Howdy, mister!" the boy called to Frank. "Where are you going? I'll trot along and hold your horse."

Frank drew back instinctively at this abrupt meeting, then, recognizing the boy and recalling his name, he drew to a slow halt saying: "Howdy, Don. How's the pup?"

Bud muttered behind him and Josh kept his horse pacing on past. This interlude did not interest him. He was thinking of hot grog at the Big Elk and that singing, big cannon stove.

"He's not so good, mister, but he's alive and he drank a little milk this morning."

"That's fine," Frank said, smiling. "Tomorrow mix the milk with some mush. Milk by itself is fine for cats, but a dog's like a man. He's got to have something that'll stick to his ribs."

From behind Frank, Bud said: "Come on. What the hell . . . ?" He reined around Frank and kneed his horse onward, throwing an impatient look at Reno, who missed this because he was still watching the boy.

"My ma says you sure did a good job bandaging him, mister. She used to be a nurse in the war an' she knows about that stuff." The boy flung a quick look upward at Given as he went on by, then returned his glance to Frank and went on speaking. "She says even my pa . . . when he was alive . . . couldn't have done a better job of fixin' a busted jaw."

"Was your pa a doctor or something?" Frank asked, for some reason he could not have adequately explained to himself, deliberately prolonging this conversation.

"No," answered Don, "he was a hospital orderly in the war. He used to tell me lots of stories."

"Used to . . . ?"

"He died two years back."

"Oh," said Frank, and searched for something else to say, but did not find the words, for a woman came onward at the roadside, holding a shawl around her shoulders, halting at the sight of them to call forward in a deeply musical way.

"Don! Donny, it's going to storm. You'd better come in now."

The boy turned, saw the woman, and said: "Ma, this here is the man who fixed my pup."

Frank raised his glance a little to look over at the woman. She was still young with black hair and a better-than-average fullness to her upper body. Her matured fullness and completeness reached out over the interval to excite Frank's male instincts. She was a handsome woman. He had no way of knowing that this was the identical woman Buck had seen earlier, and who had also stirred something in Streeter.

Then the woman smiled up at him, saying: "I'm indebted to you for what you did. Donny thinks the world of General Grant." Seeing Frank's blank look, she smiled wider, showing even, pearly teeth. "He calls the pup General Grant."

Frank made a slow and raffish smile. Then he chuckled. It was the first genuine laugh he'd enjoyed in months. "General Grant ought to be honored," he told the handsome big woman. "I guess I should be, too." He twinkled a merry look at Don. "I was in the war, too, son, for four years. And I always wanted to meet General Grant. But I never did, so I reckon I'll just settle for your General Grant."

The woman was considering Frank. She said finally: "My name is Mary Wilson." She added nothing to it.

Frank touched his hat brim with one hand. "I'm Frank Reno," he said.

"Mister Reno, could I ask you to stop and have a cup of coffee? It's the least I can do for you for what you did for Donny."

Frank put a thoughtful look up the roadway. Josh and Bud were no longer in sight. He eased forward then and swung out and down. "I'd be obliged," he said to Mary Wilson.

She walked a little to one side while Donny put up a hand to touch Frank's coat sleeve, then dropped it away, and kept pace with the older people, listening to their talk.

Mary Wilson's house was one of the little cabins that were irregularly spaced at Brigham's easternmost environs. It was, like its neighbors, neither prosperous nor well-kept looking, but, inside, there was a wealth of warmth coming from a cook stove and Frank could feel the atmosphere here, which was very foreign to anything he had known since childhood. It was an environment of love and consideration.

Donny had taken Frank's horse out to the lean-to shed. While they were alone in the house Mary Wilson became quite busy at the stove, but, when Donny entered, she turned fully toward Frank, smiling, and motioned toward a little crate.

The pup was lying there, his head swollen to half again its normal size, but its eyes bright and interested. Frank drew off his gloves, unbuttoned his coat, and knelt. The boy went down beside him. They considered General Grant quietly for a moment, then Frank reached out to put a gentle hand upon the dog. General Grant feebly wagged his tail.

"He remembers," said Donny, pleased and smiling. "He knows you, Mister Reno. He's pretty smart for being so young and all."

Frank agreed with this and stood up again.

Mary Wilson lit a table lamp. The oncoming yonder storm had deepened the gloom inside even more than outside. As she turned from this chore Frank saw once more the sturdiness of her. He also noticed that her hair was thick and tawnily black in color and matched the frank look she now gave him.

"The coffee will be ready in a moment," she murmured, moving easily from under his steady regard.

Donny sprang up, saying: "Ma, Mister Reno was a soldier, too, like Pa."

"Was he?" came Mary Wilson's quiet reply from the stove area.

Donny, boyishly exuberant, rushed on, only now turning his deep blue and sparkling gaze upon Frank. "My pa was with Sherman's Army. Which outfit were you in?"

Frank hung fire over his answer to this. He looked from the lad to his mother's back, and down to the boy again. He was quite conscious, suddenly, of an old picture in a tarnished gilt frame of a blue-eyed handsome man in a Union uniform that had a prominent place upon a shelf to one side of the stove where Mary Wilson stood.

"Sherman's Army, too?" persisted the boy.

"No," said Frank slowly. "Not Sherman's Army, son."

"Then which one?"

"The Confederate Army, Donny. Colonel Preston's Twenty-Eighth Virginia Regiment of Jubal Early's Corps."

An awkward silence settled between Frank and the boy. It extended on over where Mary Wilson's back seemed to slightly stiffen where she stood. Frank noticed this. He also saw how Donny's sparkle gradually diminished and his smile died away.

Then Mary spoke. Her words fell softly. "Donny, will you please get the cups."

The boy moved finally, turning away from Frank.

His mother twisted slightly to put her grave eyes upon the silently standing man. "Do you like your coffee black?" she asked.

Frank nodded, studying her face and finding nothing there. No expression at all except that solemn, steady look. He said: "Missus Wilson, maybe I'd better just go along. I'm obliged for your hospitality anyway, though."

She shook her head and came near to smiling quietly. "No, please stay. Donny's world is different from your world and mine, Mister Reno. He is young yet."

"Well . . . ," said Frank, not wishing to go, and twisting to see Donny standing there gravely considering him.

"Well . . ."

"The cups, Donny," said his mother, and reached out for them. "Thank you, Son." She smiled then, but not at Frank. She said: "The war was long ago, Donny. We shouldn't keep it alive."

"He was a Rebel," the boy said very softly, looking straight at Frank.

"Donny!"

Frank made a little gesture toward Mary with one hand. "Let him say it," he told her. "There's only one thing worse than keeping something bottled up inside you, ma'am, and that's hating folks."

"You hated the Union," said Donny now, his voice coming on stronger. "You were a Rebel soldier."

Frank reached back for a chair and sank down into it. He looked a moment at his hands, then he said: "Don, a soldier rarely hates his enemy. Civilians may hate the enemy, but the fighting soldier doesn't. He respects his enemy, and he's impersonal about him. He fights him, sure, because he and his enemy don't see things the same way at all . . . else they wouldn't be fighting. But I never hated Yankee soldiers. In fact, after the fight at Winchester, I carried one on my back near a mile to a Confederate field hospital. Other times, when things were slack, I traded tobacco with them for food.

"Don, men fight for the things they believe in. Your pa was a soldier and I know he was a brave one, too. I know he and I could sit down at this table now, if he was still alive, and drink coffee and talk together, because you see what he believed in proved stronger than what I believed in. But mainly we could do that now, son, because the war is far behind us."

Donny listened. He looked at his watching mother once, then swung back toward Frank. "Did you kill Union soldiers?" he asked, and as his mother made a sound in her throat, a sound of shock, Frank answered.

"I don't know whether I did or not. No man knows in a battle if he's shot anyone. But, Don, I shot at my share of 'em and sometimes it seemed like more than my share of 'em were shooting at me." He slowly smiled. "I can tell you about one time, though, when I traded shots with a Yankee. That was at Devil's Den. He was in the rocks and so was I. He'd raise up and shoot, then drop down to reload, and I'd raise up and shoot. That went on for quite a spell, Don, then I raised up to shoot, and, by golly, son, I heard someone fall . . . and when I looked down it was me!"

Donny smiled low around the lips, and his mother gave Frank a look of candid relief. Frank laughed. His teeth shone and he pushed out his right hand toward the boy.

"Shake, Don, we're friends and although friends may never see eye to eye, they can still remain friends."

Donny took Frank's hand and pumped it. He said: "You don't seem like a Rebel at all, Mister Reno."

Mary Wilson put a cup and saucer at Frank's elbow. As she poured she said: "Thank you. You did that very well."

When Frank raised his head, their eyes met and held and Mary Wilson's lips were lying closed, gently, very slightly upcurving at their outer edges. Her manner toward him was different now. He could see this at once. She approved of him as a man and did not lower her gaze from the hunger and loneliness that showed deep in his glance. They were friends. Beyond that, the interest in her glance said, it was up to Frank.

He drank the coffee feeling suddenly warm in that room. Warm in body and warm in spirit. Much of the habitual hauntedness left his face. His gaze followed Mary Wilson about the room. He thought more strongly now, that she was an extremely beautiful woman.

"Will you tell me about your side of the war sometime?" Don asked.

Frank swung and looked down. "Sure," he said, and did something he'd never before in his life done. He put out a hand to smooth tumbled hair off Donny's forehead. "Sure! I'll tell you some funny things that happened."

"Funny things?"

"Well, they're the only things that are worth remembering now, son."

CHAPTER EIGHT

John Galloway lingered in Brigham. After eating supper, he went along to the Big Elk saloon. There he had a drink and steadily watched some men playing blackjack at a table near the stove. Then he had another drink and passed on out of the saloon, crossed over to the livery barn, and engaged the night hawk there in casual conversation. This talk centered around horses, the one subject that all Westerners got around to sooner or later. The hostler had nothing to do and showed Galloway the animals in the barn.

Outside, the silently dropping snow was beginning to form dirty white edges here and there—at the edges of both plank walks, around the walls of buildings and overhead, upon store-front overhangs. But although the flakes were large and steadily coming down, as yet they formed no significant piles.

"Now these two critters," the hostler was saying as he leaned upon a stall door, "belong to a couple of stray riders that've been hangin' around town for the past few days. A week or so." The hostler looked around at Galloway. "Unusually fine animals for common cowboys to be ridin', ain't they?" Then, giving Galloway no chance to reply, the garrulous hostler said: "I know the brand . . .

belongs to the Big Springs Cattle Company way up north over the line into Montana. 'Course the Big Springs outfit runs beef into Wyoming, too. I expect them two riders probably bought these horses after they quit workin' for the company. They're as good a brace of saddle animals as I've seen in a long time."

Galloway said thoughtfully: "Men as would ride good horses like that probably got fancy outfits, too."

He watched the liveryman closely, awaiting the answer to this. The night hawk wagged his head and pushed off the door.

"Not especially," he said, and crossed over to a rack holding perhaps twenty-five saddles. "Look-a-here. These are their saddles. Nothing very special about 'em except that they sure had a lot of rough treatment."

Galloway studied the rigs. He pursed his lips and rummaged his mind for a way of getting rid of the liveryman. Finally, he said: "It's pleasant in here out of the cold. Tell you what . . . if you'll go over and fetch us back a bottle, I'll pay for it."

The hostler considered this, then smiled widely. He dropped one eyelid rakishly and said: "Stranger, you fork over the money, you plumb got yourself a drinkin' pardner."

Galloway dug in his pocket, handed across some change, then stood there as the night hawk went scuttling doorward. He waited until the man was well out into the roadway before turning, flinging loose the straps to the saddle pockets upon the rig nearest him, and plunged in his hand. He found the usual travelling cowboy's things: a straight razor, a fry pan, a change of clothing— and at the very bottom, a handful of crisp green bills. Satisfied with this find, he refastened these pockets and swiftly rummaged the bags of that second saddle. Here, he found something more tangible. It was a limp, worn, and evidently much-read letter dated a year and a half earlier from a town in Kansas, and addressed to Bud Given at a village down in Texas. Galloway read this note and then replaced it and was standing loosely at the rack, deep in thought, when the grinning liveryman returned.

They had several drinks in the livery stable office. Galloway had questions to ask: How long had Brigham had its present town marshal? What was his name? Where were the men who owned those two saddles staying? Had the night hawk ever seen them with two other men?

He inserted these questions into a long and rambling conversation, got his answers, and pressed more and more liquor upon the liveryman until he could safely depart. He then went to the hotel to ascertain if Given and Pendleton were staying there. The liveryman had not known where they were staying. But neither did the hotel night clerk. He was only certain of one thing. Neither man that Galloway was inquiring about was at the hotel.

Galloway went out onto the plank walk and stood there a long time watching snow fall and thinking his private thoughts. From their Wanted posters, he had recognized Given and Pendleton playing blackjack at the Big Elk saloon. He was satisfied his manhunt was over. But he was troubled, too. Neither Buck Streeter or Frank Reno were anywhere around and no one in town could tell him anything about them.

He ultimately put his weighing attention upon Brigham's bank and express office, across from one another, and lit a cigar he'd bought back at the saloon, feeling sardonic. Any experienced bandit like Buck Streeter would be delighted to find two such rich prizes so close together. Galloway could even imagine how the bandits would strike this town. Two of them would stand guard with the horses in the roadway and the other two would each take one of the buildings he was studying. It was the proven way of hitting a town the size of Brigham. The proven and never changing way.

The snow was beginning to build up a little now, to form soiled drifts and to eddy with a little icy breeze. Galloway smoked and stood there in darkness thinking that he had a couple of free days. He knew, as the outlaws also knew by this time, that they could not plunder Brigham until the snow diminished sufficiently to permit their afterward escape.

Galloway could accomplish a lot in two days. He could ride out, hunt up the special men Devers had sent north, and organize the surround of Brigham town using Hirt's townsmen from Shoshoni, and even some sodbusters from over Blue River way, along with the riders from roundabout cattle outfits.

He told himself fate was finally working for him, or at least she was not hindering him in his plans. Behind him a passer-by spoke casually to an oncoming dark, long, and lean shape, saying: " 'Evening, Marshal."

Galloway turned the littlest bit to sight this other lawman's face. He already knew his name— Clem Houston. But it was hard in that gloomy night to make out much more than Houston was a youngish man with droopy eyelids and an easy-going set to his mouth and jaw. *Maybe,* Galloway thought, *too easy-going*. He made a decision then and there. He would leave Brigham's town marshal out of it. He could not afford to take any chances at all. He let Houston stroll on past and watched him turn in at the Big Elk.

"A saloon lawman," he murmured to himself, making an incorrect assessment of Clem Houston, then he turned and began to walk eastward through town. He wasn't going any place in particular, but it was too cold now to stand still very long and he did not yet wish to abandon his vigil for the other members of Buck Streeter's bandit band.

He walked with a horseman's loose and easy gait as far as the plank walk went, and there he stood a moment, looking out where snowfall limited his view. He could not imagine Streeter or Reno voluntarily staying out in this weather, and a nagging doubt came to trouble him. Suppose the band had broken up. Suppose the two outlaws he wanted most had gone on, leaving the two least important ones in Brigham? Then he remembered something. The night hawk had had an answer to one of the questions Galloway had asked him. Yes, he had stated, he'd seen the two men who rode those excellent saddle horses with two other riders.

Probably then, Galloway reasoned as he turned and went pacing slowly back toward the center of town, Reno and Streeter were still around. Certainly, if they were planning a raid upon Brigham city, they'd be around. Another notion came to Galloway: Streeter and Reno might be out this very day planning the escape route. If this was so, then he hadn't arrived in town a day too early because, clearly, the band would be getting ready to strike.

He halted across from some poor-looking lighted shacks to sort the pieces of his thoughts into a kind of pattern. The outlaws would be rested now. They would feel secure from pursuit and detection down here in Wyoming. They would be working out the details of this forthcoming raid and that was why Given and Pendleton were loafing in town without Streeter and Frank Reno—because the last loose ends were being tied together, which meant, when the snowstorm passed or eased up, they'd strike.

Galloway ran the back of one hand under his longhorn mustache. He threw down his cigar and gazed intently upward. From the looks of that leaden, swollen, and dead-still sky, there would be hours and maybe even days yet of snowfall.

He became satisfied and brought his gaze downward to put it on ahead where a whiteness was beginning to limn Brigham in a square and box-like fashion. He did not like the idea of riding out, but on the other hand he knew no one here he dared trust and those special deputies from Denver had to be contacted.

He gave the heavens another searching look.

He'd chance it. He had to. He'd leave at dawn and contact the other lawmen. He'd make dead certain Brigham was so well surrounded that even a jack rabbit couldn't get through. Then, whether the Streeter gang struck or not, he'd go after them. He began walking back, and now a totally different and very pleasant thought came. He would sleep this night in an honest-to-God bed. Galloway's bear-trap mouth loosened, curved upward at its outer corners. He smiled.

Off across the unlit stretch of road past where the plank walk ended, voices came softly to Galloway over the muting hush of snowfall. He harkened to them from habit, then cast outward a careless look. A handsome, sturdy woman holding a shawl over her head and shoulders was speaking directly to a man who bulked large in a windbreaker coat. Beside the man stood a boy looking upward. As Galloway watched, the man lightly brushed the boy's head with a hand, then pulled on a pair of gloves.

The boy trotted away, bound toward a leaky-roofed old shed, and when he was gone, the man said something to the woman too low for Galloway to hear. He thought the man would bend a little, would kiss the woman. He thought they were man and wife and the boy was their child. Then, in Galloway's eyes, they did a strange thing. The woman held forth her hand. The man took it in his gloved fist and held it a moment, then let it go.

Galloway revised that earlier opinion. A man would not shake his wife's hand, he would kiss her. The lad returned leading a saddled horse. Galloway at once saw that booted Winchester, which was not standard equipment for a man riding around a town. He arrested his forward pacing to watch what ensued with a lawman's inherent curiosity.

The man turned now, tugged up his *cincha*, brushed falling snow from the saddle seat, then thrust out a hand toward the boy. They shook and something the boy said came in substance over to Galloway. Something about how quickly the man would return. Then the man mounted, tilted his hat brim to the woman, and eased his horse out past the cabin and swung westward down the roadway. He paused when he was abreast of Galloway to raise an arm and wave backward. The woman and boy returned this wave and the horseman rode on.

Galloway also resumed his forward progress. He did not look at the rider on his right again until they were both approaching the livery barn. Then, as the horseman turned in there and was momentarily illuminated by a glow from carriage lamps on each side of the stable's entrance, Galloway, remembering the stupor he'd left the night hawk in, cast an upward glance at the rider. And froze.

Frank Reno!

The rider passed inside and was lost to Galloway. He stood like stone gazing after him. Then he slowly turned and looked in the direction of that little house from which Reno had ridden out.

Frank Reno had no wife to Galloway's knowledge. He was certain he possessed no son the age of that boy. The logical assumption then occurred, but Galloway did not at once accept it. Frank Reno was not a well man. He would not in all probability waste his husbanded strength upon making love to a woman—even if he could, which Galloway doubted.

Reno had no living relatives, so far as Galloway knew. Certainly, he had none in Wyoming. Then, Galloway said to himself, it had to be that other notion. It had to be that Frank Reno had a woman.

Galloway went along toward the hotel again. He stopped beneath its wooden canopy and waited for Reno to emerge from the stable. This took quite a little wait and Galloway knew why. Then, when Reno emerged, he struck out directly for the Big Elk saloon, and Galloway, who had never before been this close to the outlaw, memorized Reno's walk, his clothing, and the way he carried his head—low, as though something was heavily upon his mind.

Reno passed out of sight into the saloon.

The snowfall suddenly increased in intensity, and John Galloway watched it for a time, seeing how it stuck now, and drifted, and eddied in the ragged wind and began eventually to sift over chuckholes and ruts in the roadway with a persistency that indicated quite clearly that it would not stop falling this night, at least, and perhaps not for another day or two.

He finally faced about and went into the hotel, nodded with—for him—unusual affability at the same clerk he'd interrogated earlier in the evening, got an upstairs front room, paid for it, and climbed upward with a little blithe lift to his steps.

Galloway never took any other than a front hotel room in strange towns. He had a long-standing habit of sitting with his booted feet cocked up, looking out over roadways as he smoked his final cigar or cigarette of the day. He did this now, feeling replete and very satisfied, and only casually watching the rare few riders pass in and out of Brigham.

He expected no more luck for one day, but he got more. He saw a stiffly riding man pass along below him with a skiff of snow upon his hat and coated shoulders. This horseman had obviously covered a considerable distance this day. Then the rider turned in at the livery barn and was limned by those same fitfully burning carriage lamps and Galloway sat straight up in his chair.

Buck Streeter!

CHAPTER NINE

Frank Reno went directly from Mary Wilson's house to the livery barn. There, he found the night hawk hopelessly drunk and had to care for his own horse. Another time this would have annoyed him. Now it did not. In fact, he was scarcely conscious of it because his mind was filled with strange new thoughts.

He afterward walked across to the Big Elk saloon, halted inside to shake snow from his shoulders, then put a searching look out over the room, located Bud and Josh at the blackjack table, and sauntered over.

Given looked up, as did Josh Pendleton. But Bud did not look down again for a time and his look spoke volumes. He said nothing, however, and went on playing cards.

Frank left to pass along to the bar. In the mirror dead ahead, he saw Brigham's town marshal talking to a woman several yards farther along the bar. He ordered some ale and stood easy, studying those two. The marshal he'd seen before. He appeared to be a Texan. He had a drowsy look to him which might have deceived some, but not Frank Reno. He had long since appraised this lawman. That was why he'd said at the band's last meeting that he doubted if Brigham's town marshal would stay clear if a fight started during the proposed robbery.

The woman with Clem Houston was small and her eyes were an unusual black-gray color. Like a gun barrel, Frank thought. Her hands where they rested upon the top of the bar were small and square. The rest of her was compactly put together and symmetrically in perfect proportion. There was something in her glance. It was not an easy thing to define. A kind of secret satisfaction as though she knew she was beautiful and that in the hungry sight of every man she was also desirable. Her assurance as much as her glance said this, as Frank studied her.

Frank shifted his attention again to the lawman. He was a man like other men, Frank thought, with all the identical impulses, and unless he was wiser about women than Frank thought he'd be, that husky little girl was going to drag him through hell. She was that kind.

The saloon was full. Townsmen with sleeve garters and cattlemen from the roundabout ranges thronged the place. It was a good crowd with no actual drunks and only a few steady drinkers. Mostly, the men talked together, now mostly about the weather, or they gambled, or passed around the room circulating in the manner of gregarious people who did not often have an opportunity to socialize.

Near the blackjack table—and the stove—

the greatest number of men stood. A man with a knife-scarred face who Frank did not know by name but who he thought was the Big Elk's proprietor, was obviously telling a joke, for when he ceased speaking, the cattlemen around him roared and winked wickedly at one another and roared again.

Frank had another ale and took it away from the bar where jostling men came and went. He went over to an empty chair near the piano player, which was on the route of men passing back and forth from the rear gambling room to the bar, and there eased down. He felt very comfortable, very loose and easy and mellow. The piano player was toying quietly with his instrument. He had a hard-top derby hat upon the back of his head and a dead cigar between his teeth. He saw Frank and leaned over to say: "Good crowd tonight."

Frank nodded, saying nothing. The piano player took this to mean Frank did not wish to converse and returned to idly plinking an occasional key.

From the nondescript flow of humanity into and out of the back room, emerged Bud Given. He stopped there, gazing downward. Then he found a chair, drew it up beside Frank, and dropped down.

"You had supper?" he asked.

Frank shook his head. "A cup of coffee and a piece of fresh-baked bread is all."

"At that kid's house?"

"Yeah."

Bud thought about this. "How come?" he said.

Frank explained about the injured pup. "The kid recognized me when we rode into town. You were there."

"Yeah."

"His mother came out. They were grateful about me bandaging up the dog. I went in an' had a cup of java and a piece of bread with 'em that the mother had just baked."

"Oh."

"The kid's pa was a Yankee soldier. He died a couple years back."

Bud stirred on the chair. Something about this talk disturbed him. He had a son, also, back in Kansas. He didn't like to think about this very often.

He said: "You reckon Buck will come here lookin' for us?"

"Yes."

"It's gettin' late though."

"No," contradicted Frank. "It's dark because of the storm. It can't be more'n seven o'clock." He tilted up his glass and emptied it of the ale, reached down and pushed the glass under his chair. "He'll be along."

"I reckon," muttered Bud, and yawned. "Frank, we can't do anything until the storm lets up."

Reno grunted. He was looking straight ahead.

There was a pensive expression around his eyes, and lower down, around his lips, there was a quiet gentleness. "There are worse towns to lie over in," he stated. "I don't care if we don't move on for a week or a month." Frank pushed his legs out to their full length and crossed them at the ankles. "Bud, do you miss your woman and kid?" he asked.

Given's gaze dulled out. He said: "That's funny talk comin' from you, Frank. Anyway, I don't want to talk about it."

Frank accepted this matter-of-factly but he was not rebuffed, he was simply driven down deeper into his own thoughts.

Then Given's voice came on again, but changed now. "Look over by the door at who just walked in."

Frank looked.

Buck Streeter stood there knocking snow from his hat against one leg. He did not at once see Frank and Bud. When he did, he shouldered through the crowd, unbuttoning his coat as he passed along. Then, when he stopped before them and looked down, he commenced tugging off his gloves.

"You boys look right comfortable," Streeter said, his steely eyes sardonic.

Reno brushed this aside, saying: "Well . . . ?"

Buck went after a chair and returned with it. He sat down and blew out a big sigh. "Too much snow building up," he commented. "But I've got the route staked out anyway."

"Still snowing hard out?" Frank asked.

Buck nodded. Bud Given looked up as a fourth shadow came out of the crowd to stop beside Streeter's chair. It was Josh Pendleton, and from his flushed look, he'd had a little more to drink than usual.

Josh bent forward to listen. Buck peered around at him.

"Too much snow piling up," he reiterated for Pendleton's benefit. "But as soon as it lets up a mite we'll go to work."

Pendleton tittered. "Suits me," he said, grinning expansively. "I'd just as soon hang around this town for a while anyway. Just won two dollars at the blackjack table."

"Big money," growled Given, and snorted. "You been drinkin' too much, Josh."

Pendleton's smile congealed. His eyes hardened against Given.

Buck Streeter, seeing this, said in a low, quick way: "Cut it out you two. Josh, stay clear of the bar. Bud, what's eating at you?"

Given said nothing. He was looking out at the crowd, through it actually, and far, far beyond it. After a while he said: "This is the last one, Buck. After Brigham I'm heading for Kansas."

Streeter's brows rolled inward a little. He shuffled his glance between the two men sitting there. "You're sure a cheerful pair tonight," he said, including Frank Reno in this. "What's eating you?"

Frank rescued Given with his reply. "Just tired, Buck. Tired to the bone and in need of a rest is all."

"All right. Hell, I told you up at that shack we'd ease off after Brigham." Streeter flung his head around. "Josh, fetch me a double shot from the bar. It's colder'n billy-be-damned out."

When Josh departed, Reno said: "It's late and that shack's going to be cold. What say we get rooms down at the Brigham hotel?"

Buck shook his head. "We're too far along. Let's not run any unnecessary risks by being too conspicuous in town."

Frank had anticipated this reply and said nothing more. Josh returned with the drink, and Streeter drank it neat, then immediately rubbed at his eyes where quick tears formed.

Off to one side of their little group someone handed the piano player some coins and he promptly hunched over his instrument banging out a dolorous wartime song called "Lorena." Somewhere, far across the room, a cowboy broke into song. Surprisingly, he had a good voice. Too, he sang "Lorena" like a man who had haunting memories of other places and other times. Much of the saloon's noise died out. Men, and women, too, grew still and many eyes sought out the singer and lingered upon him. In one way or another the Civil War had touched everyone gathered in the Big Elk this night. For most of the men it brought up solemn memories—this song called "Lorena."

Frank stirred in his chair. Across from him Streeter sat twisted half around, his hawkish profile reflecting mixed emotions as he gazed along at the singer.

Frank stood up, saying: "I can't stand any more of that." He began to move outward, through the quiet room, twisting and turning until he got to the door. There, he pushed on out into the cold night and stopped at the sidewalk's edge to let icy air touch the heat in his cheeks.

But it was not far enough. That haunting song reached out mutedly to reach down inside Frank and constrict his heart. He turned east and began walking. Around him Brigham was empty of traffic. There were lights and soft sounds but he encountered no other pedestrians. He buttoned his coat and saw how star shine was lavishing a glittering brightness upon the snow that was mounded everywhere now. For a moment this did not mean anything to him. He felt emotionally drained and filled with an inexplicable sadness that was too deep for tears.

Then he stopped suddenly, threw up his head, and swung his eyes from side to side. The overhead sky was as clear of clouds as it could be.

The moon was not yet risen, but there were the trillions of flickering little diamond-like lanterns-of-the-night—the stars.

There was no additional snow falling. There would be no more. Somehow, while he and the others had been in the saloon, that snowstorm had passed.

Everything else was swept from his mind now. He turned and studied that sky in all directions. There was a build-up of clouds over the yonder mountaintops, but he thought this must be snow banners really, not more clouds.

Eventually he lowered his head, thinking that Buck and the others should be told that the storm was past, that they need not wait longer to raid Brigham city. Then his solemn gaze went onward and outward to where warm lamplight shone upon piled snow from a window of one of those little homes on eastward from the center of town, and he became troubled. Finally, he began to wish the snow hadn't stopped.

He looked out over the mountaintops again, seeking a clue about those faintly seen billowings up there. They could be more snow clouds, he told himself. He broke off speculating. It was much too early to tell anything, and it was also much too dark.

He stood there with steam from his breath running out into the brittle night. A fresh sensation came over him. It was as though an urgency existed, as though everything in his lifetime before had fallen away and now whatever he hereafter would do, must be moved toward at once. As though all his future was being telescoped into something urgent and compelling. It was a confused and confusing sensation.

That warm square of orange lamplight winked out onward and across the snow-white road. With its going, something within Frank Reno winked out, also. He told himself he was an idiot, a fool, and worse. He was an outlaw. In six states there was a price on his head. What kind of a man was he, that imagination could get such a hold on him? What kind of a fool?

He turned his back upon that little dark house. He put his anguished look uptown where saloon lights still glowed. If what he was thinking now, in bitterness, could be put into a few words, a thought, an idea, it would simply be—too late, Frank Reno, too late. No man breaks clean with his past, not even a respectable man. An outlaw never does.

He started back toward the Big Elk saloon. In the foothills, sounding eerie this still, brittle night, a wolf bayed. This was a sound that never failed to pierce lonely men wherever they heard it. Frank was such a man. He hurried faster, each footfall striking down hard upon the boardwalk. He was still two hundred feet off when he saw

Buck and Josh and Bud Given walk out of the saloon.

They stopped at once and abruptly lifted their heads, and stood quiet until he got up to them.

"It's over," he said, and Bud looked down to shoot him a quick, probing look.

Buck Streeter looked down, also. "By golly," he said. "I'd have bet the thing would've lasted at least another day the way it was snowing."

Josh cleared his throat and spat into the snow. He buttoned his coat and said: "Come on. It'll be cold enough in that lousy shack 'thout standin' here all night."

The four of them stepped out into the roadway snow, plodding onward toward the livery barn. Off to the north those far-away snow banners over the sharply cut mountaintops were firming up into immense ragged banks of dirty clouds. Not a one of them noticed. Not even after they got astride and went stiffly and silently up out of Brigham toward the yonder plateau and the tumble-down shack up there.

CHAPTER TEN

Galloway awakened with dark night still thickly obscuring the world's finite details. He dressed and swept the back of one hand beneath his mustache and glanced out the window. It was snowing, but as he considered the drifts, i occurred to him that sometime in the night the snow must have ceased. The new flakes were smaller, too, and coming down with much less intensity. He took up his hat and left the room went downstairs, and across the deserted lobby out into the pre-dawn gloom. There, he sniffed the air and assessed the overhead sky. He had a hard decision to make. Since that earlier storm had obviously broken up and gone away, might this new storm, which lacked the other one's force, not do the same thing? And, if it did, would the Streeter band strike?

He stepped out into the roadway and watched how his booted feet instantly sank into shin-high snow. Gradually he concluded that they would not strike; not because of the fresh snowfall particularly, nor because Brigham was covered. But because their escape route would be made doubly difficult for horses, and it would be terribly cold.

He started onward across the road. He had

made his decision. At the livery barn he got his animal, saddled up, and eased down across icy leather. Thereafter, he rode out of Brigham, southbound, letting his horse choose its own gait, and in a general way, its own course of travel. He did not know the country ahead, but he knew his mount would smell hay or other animals, or even cook-fire smoke, before his rider would, and therefore he left their initial destination up to the beast.

Around Galloway the white world was bitterly cold. Less than two miles beyond Brigham he had to remove one glove, place the warm palm of that hand over his mustache to thaw the breath-formed ice particles that clung there.

Another two miles onward he felt the horse pick up speed. He eased off on the reins, let them hang and slap loosely, and the horse took him through the pit-dark, snow-lined world into a ranch yard where several lights glowed. He got to the barn and dismounted. There, four men who were saddling horses, their faces unreal and evil in guttering lamplight, straightened up and stood like stone, watching Galloway come toward them out of the darkness, trailing his horse behind him.

Finally, one of the four horsemen stepped out and said: "Howdy, Galloway."

This was Deputy U.S. Marshal Jared Black, a part-Indian officer with whom Galloway had worked before. Galloway nodded, not surprised that Devers had sent Black to work with him

"Howdy, Jared," he replied, halting. "Where are the other men from Denver?"

"I left 'em last night. One is to stay at Shoshoni The others are supposed to contact the local law at Blue River, Cutbank, as well as the big cow outfits around here, and set up a full surround."

Jared Black squinted at Galloway. "Are they still here?" He meant the Streeter band, which was obvious.

Galloway nodded. He glanced casually at the other three horsemen, saying two words about them to Jared Black: "Posse men?"

"Yeah. Not much work for 'em on the ranch this time of year. The owners let me recrui 'em for two dollars a day." Black looked at the cowboys briefly, then back to Galloway. "Before I left Shoshoni that town marshal over there, A Hirt, give us all maps of the country. We had a palaver. The others were to leave Shoshoni today at dawn. According to Hirt, they should have Brigham plumb sealed off by this afternoon at the latest. Does that sound all right to you, John?"

Galloway said that it did. He also told Jared Black he did not anticipate a raid upon Brigham at least until it stopped snowing. Then he said: "Jared, I don't like to leave town. This is the first even break we've had toward getting the Streeters."

"Why leave it then?" queried the 'breed deputy

marshal. "Go on back, John. I sure don't need you."

"I want word carried to the other deputies from Denver, Jared. I want to be damned sure there's no failure. When the posses begin moving out, they should be in some kind of communication so no one overshoots the mark or does something stupid which'll alert Streeter."

Jared Black looked steadily at Galloway for a moment. He said: "What is it, John? Did the Streeters buy off Brigham's lawman?"

Galloway hung fire over his answer to this. "I don't know," he finally said, "and I'm not going to run any risks by trying to find out. Leave Brigham's lawman out of this for now."

"I see," said Deputy Black quietly. "All right. I know how you feel. It's been a long trail for you. All right. We won't take any chance on that town marshal tipping off the Streeters. I understand what's troubling you, John, so go on back and leave the other thing to me. I'll send one of these men to pass along the word about keeping in communication." Black turned to draw his saddled animal forward. As he mounted, he said: "But you've got to get word to us what's going on in town, John. We'll set up the surround according to orders, but beyond that this'll be your show."

Galloway removed both gloves and rubbed his hands together. "Tell you what," he said. "I'll be at the hotel in town. When you've established communication with the other posses and everything is ready, send a rider to me in town. I'll send word back to you by him, Jared."

Deputy Black nodded.

Around him the cattlemen also mounted up and the last one to do so blew out the lantern before getting astride. This plunged the barn into a variety of peculiar darknesses. Star shine reflected off outside snow came in to make of each mounted, armed man a vague and ghostly silhouette.

"You learn anything of their plans?" asked Jared Black. "Are they figuring on robbing the town?"

Galloway turned to his horse, toed in, and sprang up. "I daren't ask too many questions," he answered, putting a considering look upon Black's companions. "I'll bet a year's pay, though, that they didn't come down here just for a rest. Not that bunch."

"They'd be foolish to try anything with this much snow underfoot though, John." Black eased his mount forward, up beside Galloway. "If they didn't have fresh horses cached out somewhere their animals would give out by the end of the first day."

"That doesn't worry me," responded Galloway, turning now and riding back out into the yard. "I know they can't get away this time if all the posses are alerted and waiting. What's troubling me is when they'll strike."

"Why not the army of us just ride into town, wait for 'em to show up there, then jump 'em?" said Deputy Black.

"For two reasons," exclaimed Galloway. "One, in a strange town you never know who is your friend and who is your enemy. Two, sure as hell as we did that, one or two of them would get clear of the town, and with all of us in town, they'd get away."

Jared Black grunted dourly. "They wouldn't get far," he stated. "I know this country like the inside of my hat, John. I worked cattle here as a kid. That's one reason why I came on last night instead of lying over in Shoshoni. I know the folks who own this ranch. They're old-time friends of mine. I don't give a damn where the Streeters go hereabouts, I could track them down in the dark . . . even in a snowstorm."

Galloway said: "You just might get a chance to prove that." He paused, looking thoughtful for several moments. Then: "All right. You understand how we're going to do this. I'll be waiting at the hotel. You'll send me word as soon as every road and trail is blocked off. When I feel the time is right . . . we'll go hunting for Streeter and his men. Clear?"

"Plumb clear."

Galloway nodded and eased his mount forward.

"Dead or alive," he said in parting. "Pass that along, Jared . . . dead or alive."

Black made no reply to this, but Galloway heard him talking to his posse men in that hushed, dark stillness, before he had covered a hundred yards.

Afterward, on his way back to town, Galloway thought things were going well—almost too well. He had anticipated having to scour the countryside for many miles before contacting all the men Devers had sent north from Denver. The way he had thought things would work out was altogether different from how they were working out.

He felt gratified, too, that Marshal Devers had used foresight, that he had sent Jared Black to him. Jared was a bulldog of a manhunter, and he was mercilessly efficient. When he said he'd take care of getting the surround organized, he would do it, which freed Galloway to stay in Brigham, and that, Galloway now thought, was where he should be until whatever now happened, was satisfactorily concluded.

The steady snowfall had not as yet obscured Galloway's outward imprints, and he followed these back into town. That silent, white world with its Stygian overhead canopy was smartingly cold. Riding along and at last turning a little way, at least for the moment, from this thing that had absorbed every other hour of his existence for so long, Galloway became conscious of hunger. In his active, harsh life he had never been entirely without hunger. He was the kind of a man who burnt up energy relentlessly. In consequence, he was almost invariably hungry. Yet Galloway's overpowering concentration when he was upon a trail, never allowed physical needs to interfere. Not until, as now, everything seemed to be going as planned, better, in fact, than he had planned. Then, he would think of himself, as now, and when he came back into Brigham from the south, he headed straight for the livery barn, stabled his animal without even an answering "good morning" to the day man's pleasant greeting, and walked purposefully across the road to a little lighted café. There, Galloway got around a meal that, in a country where men were large eaters, left the slovenly café proprietor in awe and vast respect for this lean, cold-eyed man with the drooping longhorn mustache.

Afterward, immeasurably gratified and replete, Galloway stood for a short while in the paling fresh new day watching Brigham come to life around him. He then went along to the Big Elk saloon, bought a handful of cigars there, and returned to his hotel room to sit cocked-back, booted feet upon the sill, smoking.

Off upon a distant hill, smoke stood straight up from an old shack Galloway could barely make out through snowfall. He thought incorrectly the place had to be either a line camp for some cow outfit, or the residence perhaps of a trapper or hunter. There was no visible corral, nor, for that matter, any sign of life whatsoever except where that rising thin plume of smoke rose upward, and even as Galloway watched, that dwindled until it quite died out.

Whoever lived up there, thought Galloway, used paper and pine kindling to get his fire lighted. That had accounted for the smoke. Afterward, he'd put dry oak into the fire box, and because dry oak was smokeless, the arrow-straight lift of smoke no longer showed.

These, to John Galloway, were idle, unimportant thoughts. The kind of things a man's mind automatically closed down upon when there was waiting to be done, or when a burden had been lifted, and his mind, out of long habit, rummaged for something else to concentrate upon.

A storekeeper came forth to whisk away any piled-up snow with a broom, and diagonally across from him a raw-boned older man, wearing mittens but no coat, stopped at the express office, worked the lock for a moment, then pushed back the door and faded out inside.

Galloway watched this particular man with some interest. He had it in his mind that this man might be dead within another twenty-four to forty-eight hours, or he might only be startled out of his wits, but however things turned out,

Galloway was dead sure of one thing. That raw-boned older man would be jarred away from his placid composure.

Brigham did not come to life all at once. In fact, the bank manager was one of the last men to come striding along, pink-faced, overly fed, and open his establishment for the new day's business. By that time Galloway had finished with his cigar and was feeling a need for coffee.

He watched the banker pass inside his building, then stood up, thinking cold and impersonal thoughts. Bank managers did not often survive raids by men like Buck Streeter. Galloway's wish for a cup of black coffee pushed this other thought into the background. He didn't care whether that banker lived or died, but he did care about some hot coffee.

He left his room, descended to the lobby, and passed outside. Snowflakes of less-than-average size were still falling, but Galloway could tell from the way they did this—flutteringly, slowly—that this other storm would shortly pass. And he didn't care about that either. Not now. Not with Jared's posse men riding over the countryside. Not with the silent army of riders stirring, fanning out, grimly turning in this fresh day to the business of writing *finis* to the wild career of four outlaws whose exploits had covered them with an aura of romanticism which, whenever Galloway had read of it in newspapers, had galled him to the quick.

He entered the same little café where he'd earlier gotten around a prodigious breakfast, saw the slovenly, fat, and raffish proprietor look at him with disbelief like a flag up in his eyes, and passed over to the counter where he dropped down, growling one word: "Coffee!"

Men began to filter into town, some in wagons, one or two in buggies, but mostly on horseback. Galloway sipped and sat cocked around looking out the window idly, his attention flicking over each passer-by and recognizing none of them. He remembered that handsome woman he'd seen Frank Reno talking to, remembered which little house they had been standing beside, and wished he dared go down there and find out what Reno had been doing there. But he didn't dare. Frank might hear of him asking questions. So he drank coffee, thinking it would probably net him nothing anyway, because, in Galloway's experience, he'd found women more loyal than men.

He turned, beckoned for a refill, and promised himself, before he rode out of Brigham, he would talk to that woman and he would find out what lay between them.

Chapter Eleven

Frank Reno was up ahead of the others, had the fire going, and had cared for the horses before Bud Given appeared in the kitchen fully clothed with his coat buttoned. He said something to Frank as Reno returned to the room with an armload of oak faggots, and put the coffee pot on. Frank stepped over Josh Pendleton, who was sprawled as though dead in his blankets upon the kitchen floor, and winked at Given. Bud looked down, his expression blank. He then helped Frank slice the fatback and fry it. Afterward, he left the house, and was gone for a time before returning.

"It's going to break up soon," he muttered to Frank, referring to the snowstorm. "But even so there's still too much of it on the ground."

Frank nodded understanding as he watched that frying meat. Josh stirred, raised his wet and slightly bloodshot eyes, caught the greasy odor of frying fatback, and turned quickly away. He dressed and kicked his blankets clear of the stove, then wordlessly left the shack and remained outside for some time. That smell of hot fat had done something queasy to his stomach. When he returned, he drank coffee but would not touch the bacon.

"Serves you right," stated Bud Given. "You never did know when to quit drinking."

Pendleton's stare turned upon Given, bright and savage, but if he meant to say anything, he did not get the chance.

Buck Streeter entered the room, took some bacon, and began to eat. He did not look at the others at all, which, Frank knew from long association, meant that Streeter had something heavy upon his mind.

After he'd eaten and was standing there, coffee cup in hand, Buck said: "It's going to quit snowing directly." He let those words lie in the silence that followed them before speaking again, his gaze moving from one face to the next face. "The route out o' here will be west, then due south. The same pattern we used up at Burnt Timbers."

"When?" Frank asked, sensing something in Streeter's look. "That's the question, Buck. Not how . . . when?"

Streeter considered the back of Reno's head a moment. "You boys are gettin' edgy," he said, as though talking to himself. Then his tone turned brisk, turned sharp. "Today."

They all faced forward looking at him.

Frank said: "In this snow, Buck? Hell's bells, there must be twelve inches of it. Without a relay of horses, we'd be afoot within three hours, riding fast."

Streeter smiled and nodded. "That's right. Maybe in less than three hours if we rode the horses hard."

"Go on."

"There's a cow outfit about three miles south of town. Beyond it, still heading south, is range country as far as I could see without any towns or ranches. West of here, there is another big cow outfit. This one has some foothill range and they've got a haystack up a little draw. There was a big band of horses eating around that stack."

"Good horses?" asked Frank, guessing Streeter's plan.

"Real good, Frank. We'll ride like hell to that stack, rope fresh animals, and go like the wind south to that other ranch, and get another relay . . ." Streeter went silent, looking around. "How's that sound?" he finally asked.

Josh shrugged. His stomach was still queasy. Bud Given poured himself more coffee, saying nothing, and Frank seemed troubled by something apart from Streeter's plan.

"You got enough blasting powder?" Buck asked Frank, and got back a nod. "Then we'll take the bank and express office today," said Buck. "And there's one thing to remember, boys. We'll have remounts," he emphasized this. "We'll have 'em. But if there's a posse after us, they won't be that lucky because we'll scatter those animals up around the haystack, and any others we run into on the way south. That way their mounts will flounder in the snow . . . not ours."

"Sounds all right to me," Given ultimately said, finishing his second cup of coffee. "Buck, you got any idea how much we'll get out of Brigham?"

Streeter's cold exuberance vanished now. With a shrug, he said: "Who knows? It's a prosperous place. That's all I can say about it."

Frank raised his head, looked outside, and began to pull on his gloves. "Let's get it over with," he muttered. "I can think of things about it I don't like, but I guess if it wasn't the weather it'd be risky some other way." He crossed past Streeter without looking at him, opened the door, and walked out of the room.

The others trooped out after him. All but Josh Pendleton had their blankets already rolled. Josh bent to this chore while the others strolled up to that secret corral, and there they waited.

Buck Streeter turned so that his cold and considering gaze lay fully upon the yonder town.

At his side, Frank said: "One thing. I met a woman and a kid in town. As we ride in, I'd like to break off for a minute or two and say good bye to them."

This brought a quick look of astonishment to the outlaw leader's face. He turned, fixing Frank with a piercing glance. "You, Frank," said Streeter in a rising tone. "You an' a woman? Well, I'll be damned."

Frank reddened. "It'll only take a minute," he murmured.

Streeter's look of surprise lingered. "I guess we can wait. If you don't take too long. Tell you what, Frank, you saddle up now and head on down there. Do Bud or Josh know where this woman lives?"

"Yes."

"All right. You ride on ahead and get your good byes said. We'll come along in a little while and get you. Josh'll be another ten minutes rolling his tack anyway."

Frank moved off and Buck watched him go. He was still watching when Frank finished rigging out, got astride, and rode on down from the plateau.

Bud Given walked over, saying: "Hey, Buck, what's Frank up to?"

"He went on ahead," murmured Streeter, "to tell some gal and a kid good bye." Buck looked around. "He said you knew where they lived. We'll pick him up on our way into town."

Given nodded, looking at Frank's diminishing figure broodingly. "I saw the kid, and I figured there'd be a woman. Yeah, I know where they live."

"What the hell's keeping Josh?" Streeter demanded, forgetting Frank Reno and turning an impatient scowl houseward.

Bud said nothing to this. He had not forgotten

Frank and leaned there now upon the corral stringers watching Reno grow small in the snowy distance.

A few infrequent snowflakes still tumbled earthward. Not many though, for the sky was beginning to lose its solid grayness. Patches of ragged clouds were breaking up. There remained that gunpowder-like grayness though. It extended from heaven to earth and filled the atmosphere making the world seem threateningly gloomy. Underfoot snow lay whitely but everywhere else was this permeating, dead grayness.

Frank moved down through the hushed morning dullness with his breath steaming outward and his eyes taking in the yonder lights, the snow-softened planes and squares, the molasses-like roadway of Brigham. There was no one abroad yet, or, if there was, he could not discern them. But straight-standing pencils of stove smoke rose up from the town and Frank had no difficulty imagining the people there sitting down to breakfast in a snug-warm kitchen, or dressing before a crackling fire, or discussing the weather as people always do when winter's first snowfall comes.

He singled out one house among those scattered dwellings at Brigham's easternmost extremity and saw how smoke also rose straight up from that residence. He could imagine what was in progress there, too. Mary would be getting Donny's breakfast; she would have his school coat and scarf and hat warming before the woodstove. She would not be thinking of anything in particular, probably, because busy people didn't. Least of all, she wouldn't be thinking of him.

His horse slipped on ice once, where Brigham's roadway began. Afterward, Frank put the animal well clear of those iced-over wagon ruts and kept him there until he came abreast of Mary Wilson's home and turned in. He rode straight on past the side entrance and to the ramshackle shed. There, he tied his horse, removed the residue hay left over from that bait of feed Donny had given the animal the day before, because, this day in particular, he did not want his horse to have a gut full. Then he slowly drew off his gloves and went forward to stand a moment looking along toward the town's heart and center.

It was too early yet for people to be much in evidence. It was peaceful standing like that, as though he lived in this town and this was his home—his family. A lonely man in a strange village, feeling nostalgia for something he had never known, could see beauty and peace and security where long-time residents saw only ugliness and insecurity, and the lonely man might wish with all his might that he belonged, while at the same time knowing full well that he would never, and could never, belong at all. Frank moved forward.

Now the last snowflakes had fallen; there remained that leaden look to the sky, to the world roundabout, and the air still smelled metallic. But those scudding clouds were breaking up faster now, being aided in this by a high, silent wind.

Frank got to the side door and knocked. He stamped snow from his feet and used his hat to beat it off his coat.

Mary opened the door. She did not appear the least surprised to see Frank there. She smiled at him and stepped aside, saying: "You're just in time for breakfast."

He entered, saw Donny at the table wriggling around to see who it was, and smiled as the lad sprang down from his chair to cry a delighted greeting to Frank.

"If you like porridge," Mary Wilson said, taking Frank's hat from him, motioning for him to remove his coat, "you're in luck. Of course, if you don't like it . . ." She looked merrily at him. "Why then you'll have to be satisfied with just coffee."

Donny took Frank's hand and led him over to the table. "It's not bad porridge," he confided. Then added: "For porridge."

Frank smiled. It was a good smile and it made his thin face gentle and handsome at the same time. "Porridge is good for a man on mornings like this," he said to the boy. "Gives him the strength he needs to get through . . . the day."

Frank ducked his head and began to eat from the bowl Mary placed before him. He looked around only once, and that was to see what Mary was doing. She was draping Frank's coat over a chair back in front of the stove. She had also put his hat and gloves there to dry. Then she came around to the table and sat across from him, saying: "Eat, Donny. You'll be late for school."

"Aw, school . . . !"

Frank looked over. Donny's deep blue eyes, clear and untroubled and innocent, showed quiet resignation and resentment.

Frank said: "Don, I want to tell you something: The day's coming when a man without schooling won't have a place in this world. He'll be a misfit. I know how that works, you see. Times change and an educated man can see the changes coming. He can change, too. But a man without schooling gets caught. He don't see the changes, and he can't change himself. So, in the end, he's a misfit. Don, there's no place in this world for misfits." Frank paused. He blinked and looked swiftly away, down at his bowl of porridge. His cheeks were faintly pink. He tried uncomfortably to finish it by saying lamely: "Well, maybe that's all sort of over your head now, Don. But you try and remember it and one day, some years from now, you'll know what I mean. Anyway, for your pa's sake . . . and for mine . . . you go to school."

Donny, sensing something here, looked perplexedly at his mother. She was looking straight at Frank. There was a deepening color to her tawny eyes. A gentle flush to her cheeks, and her lips lay parted.

"Ma," said Donny, and Mary started, looked swiftly around, and smiled.

"That's right," she said. "Now eat, honey."

They finished breakfast. Donny got into his coat, his tasseled hat, and his mittens, and he stood a moment by the door looking back at Frank. "Will you be here when I come home?" he asked.

Frank's throat closed. He forced a smile, saying: "Don't you worry, Don. We'll see each other again. Now, like your ma says, you'd better scoot." Frank took two forward steps and pushed out his hand. "Shake, son. Study hard now. Good bye, Don."

The boy shook and wrinkled his nose at Frank. "You don't call me Donny," he said, looking into Frank's face with his trusting and admiring look. "You talk to me like I was grown up."

Mary bent to kiss her son. She opened the door and gave him a little push. He called back to her a careless good bye and ran on. Mary closed the door and turned to put her back against it and her forward look upon Frank. She had both hands behind her, the way she leaned there, which threw her upper body upward and outward so that it disturbed the man over by the table watching her. She was perhaps unaware of this effect upon Frank, but her eyes never left him.

She said: "That was good bye to him, wasn't it, Mister Reno?"

"Yes'm. I'm afraid it was. This is my last day in Brigham."

"You could have just ridden on."

Frank crossed to the stove. He took up his coat and began to shrug into it. He never once took his glance from her. "No. No, ma'am, I couldn't have done that."

"Why, Mister Reno?"

Frank stuffed the dried gloves into a pocket and picked up his hat. He held it before him with both hands. "I don't expect I could explain the why, ma'am. Leastwise not so's it'd make much sense."

Mary Wilson straightened away from the door. She said: "May I try explaining for you?"

Frank nodded.

"You've never had a son. When your horse kicked his dog, you got down to help simply because he was a little boy. Afterward . . . it was something else. He was like another little boy a long way off. . . ."

"I guess that's enough," murmured Frank. "I don't like you rummaging inside me like this."

She crossed closer to him. "Why not?" she

softly asked. "People always wonder about other people."

"You might come onto something you wouldn't like," Frank said, feeling something compliant and pleasant stirring strongly within him. "Ma'am, I'm obliged for the breakfast. I got to be going along now. Ma'am . . . ?"

"Yes?"

"You take care of him."

"Yes, I will."

He was stumbling for words. He wanted to say something to her, something personal. The words would not form up. He went around her as far as the door. There, he crushed on his hat, nodded, and hastened out into the dead-gray day, hurried to his horse, and rode quickly out into the roadway.

Onward, moving ploddingly toward him, were three other riders. He waited and joined them. All four riders went along, then, leisurely, carefully, toward the center of Brigham town.

CHAPTER TWELVE

Galloway, lingering in the café after finishing his third cup of hot coffee, lit a cigar. Several men entered, ordered breakfast, ate quickly, and departed. Galloway sat on, watching Brigham town come out of its night-long hush bit by bit. He felt easy in mind and body. In fact, he felt expansive and friendly. It was this attitude that led him to nod when three familiar, roughly dressed men came in out of the cold and saw him sitting there at the counter.

These were the crewmen from his special train. They took seats down the counter from Galloway and one of them leaned far over to say in a strong whisper: "Any luck yet?"—in a conspiratorial manner.

Galloway did not reply. His thin layer of affability atrophied and he kept a hostile raw stare upon this trainman until the latter drew away, confused and red-faced, silently reprimanded by the U.S. marshal.

Galloway arose after that, tossed down a silver coin, and left the café. He stood a while upon the walkway considering a hostler across the way at the livery barn vigorously sweeping snowdrifts away from the stable's wide-mouthed doorway. He raised his glance looking upland from town, and once more sighted that tumbledown shack far off upon a little plateau that had shown smoke the night before. He thought he also saw horsemen descending the forward hill from there, but could not be sure in the uncertain gun-metal daylight and shifted his glance to the far-off mountains. There, above the highest peaks, lay a series of powdery, long clouds which were snow streamers made by a high wind creating turmoil upon those highest snow fields. The evening before, he'd thought he'd also seen that same phenomenon up there, and instead it had been more snow clouds. Now though, with somewhat better visibility, he was quite sure that those scudding high drifts were snow banners.

He considered the breaking up of the sky, the low-down and moving cloud fragments, and understood that the snowstorm was over. Another might come, of course, as the second one had the night before followed in the wake of the first storm, but he did not now consider this to be important.

The Indians had once called this country the Range of the Winter Moon. Galloway reflected upon this, while killing time, and concluded that, poetic sounds aside, it was in fact an excellent name for northern Wyoming.

A young lad in a well-worn blanket coat, tasseled hat, and mittens, went hurrying past, scuffing at the snowdrifts. Galloway saw him, caught the boy's quick and tilted look as he went by, and found his own faded, icy gaze briefly entangled in the deep, almost violet-blue eyes of this youth. Impersonally, Galloway thought the boy was a fine-looking lad, then he forgot him, as the boy hastened on by, and Galloway's attention was caught by a familiar sight.

Brigham's bank manager came hustling along, turned in at his building, and worked at the locked door before fading beyond sight inside. Galloway smiled. This morning the banker had beaten the larger and older and more sedate express company manager to work. He waited, his mind closing down around this other and belated arrival, and later, when the express company man came rolling along, his gait a mixture of the relentless onward approach of a battleship, and the serene stride of a man replete and entirely confident, Galloway's unmoving gaze turned sardonic again, turned ironic.

He watched the express company man enter his building, close the door, and raise a shade from the front window which indicated that the Overland Company was now prepared to transact business.

Galloway, a man who had never known the serenity of a well-ordered existence, briefly wondered what it must be like to constantly, over and over again, do the same things day in and day out. *Deadly,* he thought. *It must be deadly.*

He turned and began pacing slowly along toward the bank. When he was abreast of the building, he stopped to look through a window. There were three men inside. None of them looked up to observe Galloway watching them. One was donning sleeve guards of black alpaca. He was quite elderly and frail appearing. On this old man's left stood a polished big Cleveland safe with a handsome painting of the great Morgan stallion, Justin Morgan, upon the door front. Galloway's eyes flickered. Those Cleveland safes were a long shot from being bandit proof, but they certainly looked formidable.

He had the bank's interior fixed in his mind when he continued pacing along easterly. A hundred yards farther along he turned back, crossed the muddy roadway, and paused momentarily before the express company's large front window. The interior here was not entirely different. There was the same long counter— but with no grillwork above it—and there was a bookkeeper's high and tilted stand with its four-legged stool in front of it, empty now. There was no safe visible from Galloway's point of vantage, and since it was not customary for stage companies to keep much cash or bullion on hand, Galloway doubted if the safe, whichever yonder office it was in, would be as large as the bank's safe was in any case.

Express companies normally stored valuables

only overnight, seldom longer, and afterward put them upon stages which whisked them wherever they were destined to go.

Galloway also thought now that the express manager, with a bank directly across the roadway, would probably keep nothing of value in his establishment, which could be carried over to the bank for safekeeping.

He turned to resume his stroll.

A gust of knifing wind came suddenly whooping down from those northernmost snow fields. It was bitterly cold. But it fled on southward after rattling some loose roofing, a few doors and windows, and the town resumed its quiet stance in the dismal day. Galloway watched as a freight wagon, drawn by eight teams and tooled up the roadway by a bearded and blanket-wrapped driver on a high seat, responded perfectly to the teamster's one long jerk line.

This immense vehicle was given right of way by other traffic. People came to a standstill watching that jerkline driver inch his huge wagon ever closer to the plank walk in front of Brigham's general mercantile establishment. He did this with a perfection that left nothing to be desired, for, in order to swing his laden vehicle in close, he had to first cut his leaders in, and each span behind the lead horses, then cut the mount into the roadway again, and those eight teams were strung out five stores down from the mercantile building, nearly filling and blocking off the entire eastern roadway.

Then it was done, the giant brake was set, and the teamster furled his bullwhip with a flourish and grinned triumphantly at the onlookers. He climbed down with some awkwardness from that high seat, bawled for a swamper, who came tumbling down out of the wagon, too, and gave orders in a bull-bass voice for the teams to be unhitched and led away to be fed and cared for until the wagon was unloaded, which removed the offending length of horses from across the roadway.

Galloway resumed his stroll, came abreast of the hotel, and passed over through mud and snow to enter the lobby. There, where an immense woodstove loudly crackled, he turned his back to this heat and stood comfortably at ease. After a time, he drew a heavy watch forth, opened the case, glanced downward, closed the case, and repocketed his timepiece. It was close to high noon. If, under Jared Black's uncompromising insistence, the posses were getting into position, he could shortly expect to hear of this.

He went, eventually, to a chair, and sat down. But the waiting, the inactivity, the wasting sands of time began to gnaw at Galloway. He got up, stood looking out a window into the roadway with hands clasped behind him, and finally he returned to the yonder plank walk, saw Platt's barbershop, saw that it too had a wide window commanding the roadway, and moved off toward it.

There were no other patrons when Galloway entered. A tallish, thin, and graying man rose up to put aside a book and smile at Galloway. There were two leathered chairs in the shop. This man went forward to stand beside the second one, which was farthest from the window. Galloway, seeing this and ignoring it, went instead to the foremost chair, where he had an undisturbed view of the roadway, and sat down there. He removed his hat, tossed it aside, and turned under his own shirt collar. He did not remove his coat, but he did take off his gloves and fold his hands in his lap.

The barber came up to him, his smile a little forced, and said: "Shave an' haircut, stranger?"

Galloway nodded, making no reply, letting his pale eyes drift up and down the roadway again, but actually seeing very little this time because he was looking for nothing.

"Some little storm," said the barber, beginning to go to work on Galloway's shaggy head. "A mite later than last year, but one sure thing about 'em . . . they always come."

Galloway, sighting a tall form striding away from the jailhouse eastward, recognized the town marshal, Clem Houston.

He said, irrelevantly to the barber's subject:

"Your local lawman spends an awful lot of his time in the Big Elk, it seems like."

The barber took this cue easily, shifting to another topic glibly as he cut and assessed and cut some more. "He's sweet on a girl that works up there. Cute little trick named Della Watson. I expect one o' these days he'll up and marry her." The barber clicked his shears behind Galloway's head. "Nothing much for him to do anyway."

"No?"

"Naw. What's this town got bandits would want? An' the cowboys've about all drifted south for the winter. Shucks, this town's deader'n a stuffed owl in winter, mister."

Galloway digested this impassively. He kept his moving gaze upon Clem Houston until the town marshal was beyond sight. "Real peaceful little town," he murmured, and if there was a hint of something in his voice, the barber did not catch it.

"Real peaceful," he echoed Galloway. "Of course, when we get the Christmas dance organized, why then Brigham sort of comes to life. But after that . . . between New Year's Eve and the first grass, there's nothing ever happens. Like now, mister . . . the end o' the world could come and we'd hardly even notice it."

"But you get strangers here," put in Galloway.

"Yeah, we get a few strangers. But not like in summertime. Mostly they're folks passing through, headin' south . . . gettin' out o' the high country before winter really comes a-hellin' and snows us in." The barber cocked his head. "Like you, mister. Now I'd make a guess you're just passin' through."

"You'd be right," murmured Galloway.

"And I'd go further an' say you'd be headin' south."

"You might be right there, too," agreed Galloway again. This time the paleness of his eyes was a little brighter, as though in private amusement. "You just might be right there, too, barber."

"Sure I'm right. Who'd stay in the high country if he didn't have to, in wintertime? Not me, I'll tell you."

"You don't have it bad," Galloway said, loosening up a little now. "You work inside where it's warm."

"That's not the point, mister. Hereabouts the womenfolk do the hair-cuttin' in the winter. Sure, I work inside . . . only there's blessed little work for me to do until the young bucks come back into the country for the spring roundups and the summertime drives."

Galloway thought about this. It sounded plausible. He said: "Then you'd better get another trade. Something you can work at through the winters."

The barber stepped back to examine the

completed haircut. It satisfied him, so he took up a lather cup and began beating up some shaving froth. "I have a second trade," he said, as he did this. "I'm a gunsmith."

Galloway's interest rose a little. "Is that so?" he said. "Had any new customers lately?"

"Nope. Just local men." The barber moved in with his brush poised. "How's your weapon? Firin' all right? Sights tight an' lined up? I can give a Colt or Smith and Wesson the best overhaul in Wyoming, for two dollars."

Galloway said—"My gun's fine."—and closed his lips a second ahead of that descending brush, and afterward he was the barber's captive audience. He knew he had to listen, for he could not reply.

"But even the gun trade's not very rewarding around here," the barber went on, lathering Galloway generously and critically examining his longhorn mustache. "There hasn't been a gunfight in Brigham in three years. Oh, we have turkey shoots in the summer, once in a while. They're sponsored by the Grand Army of the Republic . . . you know . . . federal veterans of the war."

Galloway knew but he could not say that he did.

The barber brought out a glittering straight razor. He touched it to a hair upon his own forearm, frowned at it, then, flexing both elbows, bent over Galloway in close concentration. He made one tentative slice downward to the point of Galloway's jaw and straightened back to swipe away the lather, then he bent forward again, satisfied with the razor's cutting edge, bending to his work in earnest and talking at the same time.

"There was talk a while back of organizin' a sort of vigilance committee. Nothing ever came of it though. What do we need with a vigilance committee, I'd like to know. I scoffed it down when the fellers'd come in to get their shaves and haircuts, and it came to nothing."

The barber drew back to wipe off more lather from his razor. Then he went off on a fresh tangent. "You know," he confided to Galloway, "a feller'd be surprised how much influence a town barber has. He gets just about all the merchants and substantial men in his chair every month or two, and if he's the only barber in town like I am, by golly, you'd be surprised how much influence he has."

Galloway's face was wiped clean with a warm towel. He sat up to say dryly: "Yeah, I can imagine." He swung to look at himself in the rear mirror. He looked quite presentable. More presentable in fact than he'd looked in months.

The barber came toward him with a bottle of French toilet water poised. Galloway ducked away from this by rising up from the chair. He brought forth a small coin and handed it over saying: "Save that stuff for those young bucks you were talking about, I don't need it."

"It's imported," protested the barber.

"That's fine, only I don't want to smell like any sporting house, so just pour my share over the next preening rooster you get in here."

The barber shrugged.

Galloway looked at himself again in the mirror, nodded to the barber, and walked on out of the shop, hat in hand.

Cold air hit him in the back of the head and down along the neck where there no longer was any hair. He put on his hat and started back toward the hotel lobby. As he paced along, Galloway took out his timepiece again, consulted its spidery little hands, and pocketed it.

Any time now that arranged for messenger from Jared Black would be riding in.

He looked indifferently up the roadway and out across to the far side. Brigham was as usual, quietly, thriftily going about its business.

Galloway turned into the hotel, failing to see four riders coming along from the east because that high-seated and enormous freight wagon at the mercantile store hid them from him. He was thinking now of having a noonday meal.

CHAPTER THIRTEEN

Streeter put a look over at Frank, and Reno drew rein so that Buck and Josh Pendleton rode a little ahead of Frank and Bud Given as they progressed down through Brigham traveling westerly. It looked less conspicuous, two pairs of riders each, instead of four horsemen abreast. They always hit towns in this fashion anyway—Streeter and Pendleton on ahead, Reno and Bud Given farther back. It facilitated what came next.

Buck pushed leisurely along as far as the hitch rack in front of the bank. There, he dismounted. Josh also swung down there, and both men looped their lines—did not tie them.

As they were moving through dirty snow and mud toward the plank walk, Frank and Bud came to the same rack and dismounted to loop their lines also.

Except for the fact that those four standing horses had carbine butts jutting upward, forward of each saddle swell, and light bedrolls lashed aft of each cantle, their animals looked about like any of the other horses tied along Brigham's main thoroughfare.

Frank strolled up beside Streeter, saying in a quiet tone: "Wish we'd gotten here when that freighter had its jerk-line hitch blocking the roadway."

Streeter nodded in silence. He was making a careful survey of the town, taking its figurative pulse. When this was completed, he said in the same quiet voice: "Go buy a stage ticket. I'll go cash a bill at the bank. Meet you back here."

Frank looked briefly at Bud and Josh. Pendleton's pale face was indifferent, but Given—and Reno had noticed this in Bud before—had a shiny sweat upon his forehead. He moved off, went across the road, and entered the Overland Company building.

At once a tall, raw-boned older man came to him from behind the counter and Frank had only a moment to select his pseudo destination from the printed stage schedule before the older man said: "Where to?"

"Cutbank," replied Frank, and tendered a crisp bill.

"Three dollars. The stage'll leave here about one o'clock."

Frank got his change and his ticket. He pocketed both and nodded at the older man. "Hope the road is open," he said.

The office manager shrugged. "If it wasn't we'd have heard by now. Thank you." He turned away and moved off, leaving Frank standing alone considering the office.

There was no safe visible, but this meant

nothing. The old man seemed to be entirely alone in the office. This bothered Frank because there were other desks and tables and even two closed office doors, indicating that the normal complement here was at the least three persons. He finished his examination and returned to the plank walk. Across the way Bud and Josh still stood where he had left them, near the horses and alert, but Streeter was not with them. Frank moved out.

When he got back across the road, Bud said to him: "All right?"

"I reckon," muttered Frank. "There's one old man in there an' there should be at least three people. But I don't suppose that's important."

"It isn't," stated Josh. "I like 'em better when there's only one feller to watch." He looked up and down the road. "Wonder where that damned town lawman is?"

"In the Big Elk," guessed Frank.

"He'll come boilin' out, more'n likely."

"Not unless something goes wrong and we have to shoot."

"Hell, there's always shooting," growled Pendleton. "But don't worry, I'll be watching for that bird. That slug I got in the calf of the leg over in Oregon has sort of learnt me to keep an eagle eye on these cow town marshals."

"What," mumbled Given, "is taking Buck so long?"

Frank did not speak. He was viewing the town over the high sides of that parked freight wagon. It occurred to him that if anything *did* go wrong, that freighter would prove a godsend. Fifty men could hide behind it and be perfectly safe from gunfire directed toward them. He turned, ran a thoughtful glance easterly. *Unless,* he thought, *the gunfire comes from that direction . . . then there will be no protection at all.*

This was all a familiar pattern to Frank. He'd survived more of these slashing raids than he cared to recall. But now something jarred him. On eastward, the way he was gazing, lay the home of Mary and Donny Wilson. At this moment though, such a recollection had no place at all in his thoughts. He fought it down and turned very deliberately to gaze at the bank.

Buck Streeter was just emerging. He was pushing a wad of bills into a trouser pocket. He looked up, caught Frank's eye, and slowly, knowingly, dropped one eyelid. Then he strolled on over where the other outlaws were waiting.

Josh Pendleton grumbled: "It took you long enough, Buck."

Streeter ignored this. He looked at Bud, then on to Frank. "Like Burnt Timbers," he said. "Only better. What did you see, Frank?"

Reno related exactly what he'd encountered at the express office.

Streeter, looking slightly flushed, slightly high

in spirits, said: "You got that dynamite under your coat, Frank?" Reno nodded. "Good. Then go have a look at the bank. Get some change like I did. The bank's yours, anyway. I'll go buy a stage ticket."

"To Cutbank," said Frank, and started past Josh Pendleton towards the bank's front door.

As Frank was entering the bank a dog fight broke out in front of the livery barn. He turned on the threshold to see this. A hostler ran out with a broom to break it up, but across the way, in front of the Big Elk saloon, a massively built big teamster with a fabulous beard roared in his bull-bass voice: "Leave 'em be. Let 'em fight it out, dammit!" And the liveryman stopped to stand there dubiously considering the fighting animals. The teamster held aloft one huge hand in which was coiled a rawhide bullwhip.

"Two dollars on the yeller cur," he challenged. "Two dollars cash on the yeller cur fer whippin' the black one!"

Frank entered the bank. Somewhere behind him a man laughed and shouted that he'd take the teamster's bet. There were other voices, too, but Frank did not heed them. He crossed to a grilled place at the bank counter and held forth a twenty-dollar bill. To the waiting man behind that grillwork, he said: "I'd like this broken down into ones and fives if you would."

The clerk took the twenty and crinkled his eyes

at Frank as he deftly made the change. "You're the second one in the past few minutes," he said. "Must be a helluva poker game going on somewhere."

Frank smiled, took the change, put his lightning-sharp gaze over that big Cleveland safe, recognized its style and its weaknesses instantly from having blown others of the same kind, and left the bank with an indelible imprint in his mind of how the room looked, where the employees were, and even the number of customers in there.

When he got back to the others, Buck Streeter was crossing toward them over the roadway. Frank said nothing until they were all together again, then he said: "It'll be noon directly. Folks'll be sitting down to dinner. Let's wait for that." At Buck's steady look, Frank said: "There are too many people in that bank. There'll likely be only the three employees when it's noon."

Streeter nodded finally, with some semblance of reluctance over the delay, but he said nothing contradictory. "All right, we'll wait," he stated, then looked at Josh and Bud. "That express company is a cinch. One old duffer in there and that's all."

"But," said Given, speaking up now for the first time, "the point is . . . is there any money in there? Look, Buck, it's smack-dab across the road from the bank."

Streeter understood and raised his shoulders,

then let them fall. "What's the difference?" he responded. "If I don't get it from the express office, Frank'll get it from the bank. Either way we'll get it."

Bud now said: "You'd better let me go along with Frank. Josh can mind the horses alone. He's done it before. If anything breaks I can run back out here right quick anyway."

Streeter put a cold look upon Given. "Seems to me," he drawled, "that there's gettin' to be too many leaders in this band." Then he went quiet.

Given lowered his head, saying nothing more.

Frank though was not cowed. "I like Bud's idea, Buck. I think there's quite a haul in that bank, and if there is, a one-handed man isn't going to run out with more than one bagful. Bud can cover me from beside the door, and I'll bring out the loot."

"Dammit," ground out Streeter, his steely eyes burning against Frank now, too. "*I* give the orders. We all agreed on that a long time ago down in Texas, and nothing's happened to change it."

"All right," Frank said quietly. "All right, Buck. I was just figuring that we risk our hides. We risk 'em just as much for one bagful of money as for three or four. That's all."

There was a kind of logic in this to arrest Streeter's increasing irritation, and there was also enough to excite his greed. "I don't like leavin' just one man with the horses, though," he muttered. "Supposin' something goes wrong? Supposin' he gets shot?"

"The horses will still be there, Buck."

Streeter fell briefly silent again. Then he mumbled: "All right, Frank. Take Bud with you."

Josh Pendleton began to frown immediately. He did not like this last-minute change. Streeter, understanding, said to Pendleton: "I'll quit the express office as soon as I can and get over to stand by you, Josh." Pendleton did not look particularly appeased by this declaration, but he mumbled assent to it.

From the corner of his mouth Bud Given said— "The marshal."—and slowly each head turned to look beyond that freight wagon, where men were at work unloading, to see Clem Houston standing idly upon the plank walk in front of the Big Elk, picking his teeth with a toothpick, gazing serenely over the town. He seemed a picture of a man who, having just eaten his fill, was considering what unimportant thing he would do next.

Streeter scoffed in a low way. "Cow town lawman. Josh'll whittle him down to size if he gets in the way."

Pendleton muttered assent to this, then added: "See that tall feller with his back to us, walking west there towards the café? I've seen him before."

"Yes, you have," stated Frank, also watching the farther figure. "He was in the Big Elk yesterday while you and Bud were playing blackjack. What of it?"

Josh looked uncomfortable. "Nothing. I got a feelin' I've seen him somewhere before, is all. You don't see many of those Texas longhorn mustaches around anymore. Specially this far north."

Frank though, watching the far-away stranger push into the café, considered him unimportant, and let the conversation about him end there.

"How long we goin' to stand here?" Bud Given demanded. "Let's get it over with."

"Plenty of time," replied Streeter, putting his deliberate glance upon Given. "Like Frank said . . . let 'em all get sat down at a dinner table . . . then we'll put it off. And, Bud . . ."

"Yeah?"

"You an' Josh remember . . . no shooting unless these fools shoot first. We don't want to raise hell an' prop it up unless we have to."

Given looked stung by this. He said, with spirit: "Buck, by God, any day you don't think I hold my end up in these raids, you just say so."

"Easy," said Reno. "Easy, Bud. Leave him alone, Buck."

Josh took out a tobacco sack and methodically went to work building a cigarette. He lit it, exhaled, and said as he glanced along the roadway: "Yonder goes some old gaffer from the express office. Buck? Wasn't there no shotgun man in there?"

"No."

"Well, that old gaffer didn't lock the front door so someone must be in there now. Want me to saunter over and look in?"

Streeter growled, "No. If there's an armed guard in there, it won't make any difference." He looked across at Frank. "Now," he said. "Frank, let's get going."

"Hold it," Frank said sharply. "Let that damned lawman walk away. He's still standing there suckin' his damned teeth."

They were getting edgy, particularly Bud Given whose face glistened with cold sweat and whose sucked-in flat mouth was a bloodless line across his lower face.

Josh Pendleton swore, saying: "To hell with him, Frank. This standin' here waitin' is worse'n being shot at. Let's move!"

But Frank and Buck were both standing like stone, their onward stares fixed upon Clem Houston. As long as they remained rooted, the others did not move either.

Then the town marshal turned upon his heel and started westward down the plank walk. A hundred yards along he stepped down into the soupy roadway, passed across it to the other walkway, and proceeded onward to his jailhouse. There, he disappeared inside.

Buck Streeter drew in a breath, turned, looked at the others, then faced fully around so that his outward stare was fully upon the express office. "All right," he said in an almost conversational tone, "let's go."

Streeter stepped down into the roadway, steadily walking. Frank and Bud moved out away from Josh Pendleton, also steadily walking. Josh watched them all depart, then he went forward to the hitch rack, freed four sets of looped reins, and got in between two horses. There, he stood motionless with his right hand lying lightly but firmly upon his holstered gun.

CHAPTER FOURTEEN

U.S. Marshal John Galloway fidgeted where he sat sprawled in the hotel lobby. It was past one o'clock. Doubts assailed him. Supposing the Streeter gang did not ride into town today? Suppose they had moved on, or had become suspicious, someway? No, he kept saying to himself, none of these things had happened. How could they become suspicious? They could not have encountered any of the posse men yet, surely, and everything else was as it had been. No, they were still around.

The trouble was—he did not know where. If he'd possessed that information he'd have brought up the posses and attacked them in their camp.

He got up, lit a cigar, and paced once up the lobby's length, and once down it. Then he saw the clerk watching him with interest, swore under his breath, and went to stand before the lobby's front window, looking out. Men were staggering into the mercantile store under burdens taken from that gigantic freight wagon. He watched this for a while, then looked beyond the wagon. Since those high sides obscured his vision in that direction, and also because there was nothing to see up there but some cowboys, four of them standing idly with their backs to him, talking, he looked westward. Here, his interest was instantly arrested. A solitary rider was plodding steadily toward the hotel hitch rack. Even as Galloway watched, this man, who he had never seen before, turned in, stepped down, and tied up.

The man was chewing a piece of wood, a long splinter. As his jaws moved easily, this stranger turned and ran a quiet glance over the town, then he turned about and stepped up onto the plank walk, crossed it, and entered the hotel.

Galloway also turned, but continued to stand there by the window, watching this stranger pause and put a searching, slow glance roundabout. When he saw Galloway, he considered him with a bold gaze for several seconds before crossing over toward him.

"Howdy," this stranger said quietly. "I don't see but one longhorn mustache in the room. Mind if I ask your name, mister?"

"I don't mind," answered Galloway in the same quiet way. "It's U.S. Marshal John Galloway. Does that answer you?"

The stranger nodded. "It does," he said. "I'm Pete Wright. I was in the barn this morning when you rode out an' met Jared Black. I didn't get a good look at you then. Too dark, Mister Galloway."

"Never mind that," said Galloway. "Did Jared send you?"

"Yes, sir. I'm to tell you Marshal Hirt's in place from north to south between here an' Blue River with forty men . . . thirty from Shoshoni an' ten from Blue River."

"That sounds escape-proof."

"Yeah. An' I'm also to tell you a deputy marshal named Frank Belanger, who come up from Denver with Jared, has twenty-five more posse men strung out from south o' Blue River on west to Circle Ten."

"I don't know the Circle Ten," stated Galloway.

Wright nodded, not surprised. He said: "It's a big ranch mostly west of Brigham, but its range also goes a considerable way south, too. Mostly though, its land lies along the foothills. They feed up against them hills for protection against storms. They put up stacks o' hay in the little protected cañons and . . ."

"I'm not interested in haystacks," spat Galloway, irritated by this cowboy's phlegmatism.

Pete Wright nodded again, accepting this rebuff. "Anyway, this here Belanger feller's posse has the southern escape route sealed off from where his line joins Hirt's line to Circle Ten."

"Where is Jared, then?"

"He's got sixteen men, including me. We're south on the range to where Belanger's last riders are standing by, an' from there we go plumb north to the foothills, then on west again, up behind Brigham. Jared hisself is at a little trapper's shack on that little plateau you can see northeast o' town here."

Recalling this cabin, Galloway said: "I know the place. Never been up there but I've seen it from town."

The cowboy brought forth a crumpled paper and held it out mutely. Galloway looked down, took the paper, and unfolded it. The cowboy now said: "Jared wouldn't write you no note, Mister Galloway. He said he didn't want to run no risks. But he said you'd understand what he wanted to tell you from that paper."

Galloway took the scrap of paper to a spittoon and dropped it there. He scrupulously wiped his hands afterward. "I understand," he said, when he went back where the cowboy waited. "That was an old scrap of newspaper."

"Yeah, I know. I saw it."

"It had blood on it."

"Yeah. Like someone spit blood on it."

Galloway went quiet, thinking that now he knew where the Streeter band had holed up, and also thinking dourly that if he'd known that earlier, since that shack was located upon a prominent eminence free of brush, he could have surrounded it and brought down the outlaws very easily, probably in one big volley of gunfire.

The cowboy broke in to scatter these thoughts, saying: "Jared wants instructions. He says ain't no one but him up at the shack now, an' ain't no

157

one he's talked to seen or heard of four mounted strangers loose in the land hereabouts. He wants to know what you figure for him to do."

"Go back," directed Galloway, "and tell Jared to rest easy. The Streeters will either come on into town, or they'll go back to that shack. Tell him to bring up three or four good men to stay at the shack with him. Tell him, just in case they *do* return, not to light any fires and to hide his horses. You got all that?"

"Yes, sir."

"Then go on back."

"Yes, sir."

The cowboy turned and passed across the lobby, went over to his mount at the hitch rack, and was in the act of untying him, which Galloway was watching from the hotel window, when Brigham's town marshal came strolling along, on his way to the Big Elk, and stopped to call out: "Howdy, Pete! You picked a helluva day to ride into town."

Galloway distinctly heard Pete Wright's casual reply to this. "Oh, it ain't a pleasure ride, Clem. It's this posse business."

Galloway turned cold at this. He saw Clem Houston, in the act of striding on, come to a sharp, quick halt and turn an abrupt stare at the cowboy. "What posse business?" Houston sang out.

"That U.S. marshal business," replied the

cowboy, turning to mount his horse. "You know, Clem. Them Streeters."

Now Town Marshal Houston moved swiftly down off the plank walk into the roadway's icy slush. He caught Pete Wright's reins and held them tightly. "What the hell are you talkin' about?" he demanded in a rising way.

Wright, settling over leather, looked down perplexedly. "Let go my reins, Clem," he said in puzzled protest. "You know, dammit. That there U.S. marshal in the hotel . . . I'm part of his posse. The whole town is surrounded by us posse men. We're waitin' for those Streeters to show themselves."

Houston released the reins. He was staring upward. "There's a federal lawman in the hotel?"

Wright's perplexity deepened. He said roughly: "Didn't you know, Clem? Sure, he's a lean-lookin' feller with one o' them old-fashioned Texas longhorn mustaches. His name is Galloway."

Houston stepped clear as Pete Wright turned his horse.

Wright said: "I got to get back, Clem. Go on inside, if you want to, and hunt up that Galloway feller."

Galloway moved clear of the window. He was angry, yes, but more than that he was fearful. Going over by the lobby door, he positioned himself beside it and back a little, so that when

Houston entered he would be behind him.

Houston came into the lobby with quick, hard steps. He stopped short and flung outward his rummaging gaze. From behind him, Galloway spoke up: "Steady, Marshal. I'm behind you. Don't do anything rash."

Houston turned. His droopy lids were down and narrowed. "Who the hell are you?" he demanded.

Galloway identified himself.

"What's this talk about a surround and a posse and the Streeter gang?"

Galloway explained these things, too, his voice quiet, cold, and inflectionless. Then he said to Clem Houston: "I've been trailin' these men too long and too far to risk anything, Marshal, and in strange towns I don't always contact local lawmen. In my experience I've been sold out a few times. That's not going to happen here."

Houston stood a moment staring at Galloway. He ultimately reached up, pushed back his hat, and scratched his forehead. His face crumpled into a bitter frown. "I'll be doubly damned," he said in an altered tone. "You worked all this without a leak."

"Not quite, Marshal. That cowboy told you about it."

"Yeah, but too late, Mister Galloway. Even if I was in with the Streeters, it'd be too late for me to do anything."

"No," said Galloway. "You could jolly me a

160

ittle . . . like right now . . . then turn and walk out o' here and send them word."

Clem Houston's eyes widened, took in Galloway's easy stance, his dangling right hand within inches of his lashed-down six-gun, and, understanding, came closer slowly but solidly. "Marshal Galloway," he said, his voice fading out low, "I've heard of you. I've heard it said you operate without the law as much as within it to get your men. I don't approve of that exactly, but I can understand it. But here in my town, Marshal, I'd walk a little softly if I were you."

"Oh?" said Galloway, and showed Houston a wintery small smile. "Now you've had your say, so I'll have mine. You look like an honest man, Houston. You make a good impression on me. But like I just said, I've sweated and froze too long to lose Buck Streeter, Frank Reno, Josh Pendleton, and Bud Given now. Because I'm inclined to distrust a man I never saw before I came here, and never in my life talked to until this damned minute, doesn't change a damned thing."

"All right!" exclaimed Houston. "What've you got in mind?"

But Galloway—although he had an idea—turned this query about, giving it back to Houston. "You," he said, "tell me what you'd do in my place."

"I'd keep you with me," Houston answered at

once. "I'd not let you out of my damned sight until I was satisfied about you."

"Or until the Streeters struck," murmured Galloway, thinking about this and beginning to like it. "All right, Marshal Houston, that's what we'll do."

"Wait a minute," said Houston sharply. "You said until the Streeters struck. Are they *here?*"

"Yes."

"And you're sayin' they mean to hit my town?"

"I'm confident of that, yes."

Clem Houston half turned away from Galloway. He looked with a smoky gaze out the hotel window into the yonder roadway. He breathed: "I'll be doubly damned."

Galloway's little wintery smile now showed some genuine amusement. "You're either one hell of a good actor," he declared, "or else I brought this off better than I expected. Marshal?"

"Yeah?"

"I was just fixin' to go get something to eat. Some dinner. I'd admire to have you join me."

Houston faced back again. His gaze was brooding and troubled. "You plumb certain? I mean, did you actually trail 'em here to Brigham?"

"I did. All the way from Burnt Timbers, Montana, where they robbed a safe and made off clean with a pretty big haul. They went over the two mountain ranges between here and there, lost he pursuit, and been campin' in an old shack on a little plateau overlookin' your town for about a week now."

"Hell, the Streeter band . . ."

"Yes," said Galloway. "Now then, Mister Houston, if you'll just walk out o' here ahead of me and mosey along the sidewalk westerly to the first little café, we can have a little dinner and discuss this."

Galloway waited, keeping his pale gaze full upon Town Marshal Houston. When the latter finally turned and moved out, Galloway fell in behind him. In this fashion they passed outside and went along westward down the plank walk with Galloway's back nearly hiding the onward-pacing form of Clem Houston.

Inside the café, they took a table well away from other diners. Houston unbuttoned his coat, put aside his hat, and leaned forward to clasp his hands and gaze at Galloway.

"How big is your surround?" he asked.

"A complete circle. It runs north to south between here and Blue River, then east to west and on from the west to the north again, curving plumb around your town. The only part of it which is open is due north from town. There's no need for men up there, if the Streeters are inside my surround . . . and I'm positive that they are . . . they couldn't get back over those mountains because of snowdrifts anyway."

Clem Houston leaned back in his chair. "Wha beats me though," he muttered, "is how yo managed to accomplish this without me hearin about it."

"I had to," answered Galloway. Then he thought a moment, and changed this. "Well maybe I didn't really have to, Marshal Houston Maybe I just thought I had to play the cards close to my chest. Like I said, though, I've run across bought-off town marshals before. I couldn' take that chance this time. Marshal, it's nothing personal. Believe that. I just didn't know, and I just couldn't take the chance. You understand?"

"I understand," Houston said, then twisted as the café man came up to take their orders.

Chapter Fifteen

Frank Reno was not consciously nervous as he stepped inside the bank, unbuttoned his coat, and swept back the hanging cloth so that it was hitched into his gun belt safely clear of his holstered gun.

Bud Given was behind Frank, a little to his left and with his shoulders against the wall beside the doorway. Bud's face was gray, which made his eyes appear larger and darker than they were.

Frank appraised the room. A woman and a man were standing relaxed at the counter. The old man with those black alpaca sleeve guards was perched on a stool at his ledger desk next to the Cleveland safe. The old man had a topless green eye shade on. His hunched, old, and bony back was faced away from the pair of outlaws.

There were two other men behind the counter. One was a short, cherubic-looking man—the bank manager. The other person was a clerk. He was finishing with those two customers.

Frank glided two steps closer to Bud, and said gently: "Let the man and woman leave first." Then he sauntered forward to take a position behind the two customers. Finally, the two turned and walked doorward. Frank now stepped up.

The clerk looked at him, a flicker of recognition showed.

"You lose that twenty dollars already?" he asked genially.

And Frank answered with no hint of responding joviality at all. "No, I didn't lose it, mister. I just need a lot more to go with it is all." Then Frank drew his gun and put it up high. He cocked it. "Put both your hands on the counter and keep quiet," he directed.

The bank clerk's blue eyes widened and widened. He had a round soft face with no amount of character in it, and he was gradually very afraid as he stared in fascination at the wasted, lean, and weathered countenance across from him.

"Now turn around," said Frank. He struck him down hard in an overhand short arc before the turn was completed. The clerk crumpled without an outcry. His falling body made a small rustling sound.

Frank passed around the counter, leveled his gun at the fat-faced younger man and raised his voice, saying to Bud Given: "Close the door. Draw that blind."

Bud obeyed, and as he did so the bank's other two employees twisted at the sound of Frank's voice—and froze.

Frank wig-wagged his gun, saying to the fat young man: "Open the safe."

The man's eyes bulged. He had small features pushed up close together in the pink roundness of his countenance. He did not look like much of a man. He stood there, staring and not moving.

Frank centered his weapon.

"I said open that safe."

"I can't," the fat man squeaked. "I swear to you I can't. It's locked at eleven and the timer on the clock doesn't open it until three."

Frank knew Cleveland safes. They had time locks all right, but he'd never heard of one being time locked in this fashion before. "You're lying," he said. "Mister, this is no time to lie."

"I swear to God," gasped the fat man. "We have definite orders to lock that safe every day at eleven and set the clock for three in the afternoon. It's a safety precaution. The bank directors say most hold-ups occur about noon. They said even without hold-ups dinnertime is a weak spot in the day. Folks go out to . . ."

"Shut up and sit down!"

The shaken bank manager snapped his girlish lips and dropped back into a chair. Frank looked across at the old bookkeeper.

"Get over by your boss," he ordered. "I'm going to blow that safe."

The old man scrambled down off his high stool with astonishing agility and glided clear.

"Bud, how does it look out there?"

Given twisted to peer out the door. "All right so far!" he called back. "Josh is ready."

"Buck?"

"No. Not yet. But it looks quiet over there."

"Keep watch while I set my charges. Keep me informed."

"Yeah. You bet, Frank."

"Keep a gun on these two."

"I will."

Frank put up his gun, reached inside his coat and brought forth three taped-together partial sticks of dynamite. He ignored the eyes of the silent and terrified bank employees and went to work setting this charge, splicing in a fuse, and running it back far enough so that he would be safely away when the explosion came. As he hunkered there behind the counter, he looked up. Fat-face and the old bookkeeper were staring at him, as white as new linen.

Frank said to them: "Boys, you can save us all some trouble if you'll open that thing."

The young man's mouth opened but no words came forth. The older man said shakily: "He warn't lying, mister. She's set for three and can't no power this side o' heaven open her afore that time."

Frank struck a match and held it so they could both see it. "I can. I'm a power this side o' heaven that can open it, old-timer. You fellers turn your faces away. Better turn your chairs plumb

168

around. The blast probably won't injure you, but the shock's been known to collapse a man's skull." He paused a moment, listening, then he called out: "All right, Bud?"

Given's answer did not immediately come back. "All right, Frank. Still don't see Buck, but the place is quiet out there."

"You got the door unlocked?"

"Yeah. And my gun ready, too. Let her go, Frank."

"Josh all set? The horses loose? The way out clear?"

"God dammit, Frank, I said all right!"

Reno lowered the match. Instantly there came a sputtering, a loud hissing, and a little moving shower of sparks. He lifted his head, putting a steady look onward down the room where the old man and the bank manager were watching.

The old man moved at once, as soon as Frank lighted that fuse. He scuttled well back toward a corner and dragged up a chair, backward, in front of him, its solid wooden back in front of his chest, shoulders, and head. Frank thought the old man had been through this before. He knew what those shock waves could do.

But the fat young man did not react at all as Frank had expected. He sat forward in his chair, bracing into the actual reality of this thing that was happening to his bank, stiffened by something inside him which was almost—but not quite—manly courage.

Frank watched him struggle with his courage, saw him waver forward and back, uncertain, unequal to this issue. Sweat broke out in large drops upon the fat man's face.

Frank knew there would be an accompanying weakness in his belly, in his legs, to go with this sweat. Then he saw the man's fear triumph, saw his manhood dissolve and run out of him like water. Saw the strange putty look around his mouth and knew that this young man had plumbed the depths of his bravery and had found himself wanting, and would forever after know self-hate and feel himself unequal in the company of other men.

He looked down, as soon as he was sure the young man would not be heroic, and saw that the fuse was very close to those set charges in the big safe's recessed door. He scuttled around behind the counter, pulled his head down, and covered his neck with both hands. He did not look to see what Given was doing. He had no time. The explosion went off with a crashing great impact as of thunder. Dust came out of the walls, the ceiling, even the floor.

Frank sprang up, running. He got through to the safe, kicked savagely at a torn dagger of extruded steel which had been a portion of that flung-away door, and dropped to his knees, hands plunging on into the belly of that wrecked steel box.

"How is it?" cried out Bud Given from beyond the counter. "Frank? What's it look like?"

"Good," sang out Reno, fighting down a terrible cough and blinking his eyes in the smoke and dust. He was filling two sacks from a coat pocket with packets of paper money, stuffing them in at random, losing some loose bills as he did this, and frantically thrusting aside some leather sacks of coins. He worked swiftly and efficiently, mostly by feel because of the smoke. Then he had both sacks full and was moving back, straightening up, and whirling away.

Outside, there rose up a quick, sharp peal of alarm.

Frank moved away from the safe and back to Bud, gasping: "Open it, open it!"—meaning the door. Given wrenched fiercely and the outside afternoon air, rawly cold and clear as glass, rushed at them.

"Buck!" Given cried out to Frank as they rushed toward Josh and the horses. "Buck . . . out here in the road!"

Frank flung the tied sacks around his saddle horn and tore loose his reins from Josh's fingers. He fought his mount around and was getting up when a gunshot sounded, then two more gunshots, all coming from westerly along the plank walk.

"It's Buck!"

He was bumped by Josh, who was also scrambling into the saddle. Josh stiffened as yet another gunshot came, then he let off a loud curse, raised his hand gun, took deliberate aim past Frank's shoulder, and fired. Frank winced, dropped low for a rearward look, and saw two men standing clear of the plank walk in front of a café.

One of them took Josh's slug high in the body. He was rubber-legged as Frank watched. He let go his gun, put out both arms as though to ward off something, then he went over forward to fall face down and full length in the filthy snow-water mud. He did not move again. The remaining man had a drooping longhorn mustache. He was standing wide-legged, firing.

Frank heard Given cry out Streeter's name twice more.

"Buck! Buck!"

Frank had only time enough to hear the anguish in Bud's cry, then Josh aimed calmly and fired again past his shoulder. He saw, from a corner of his eye, that wide-legged, mustached man go down as though someone had kicked both legs from under him. He broke his fall with an outflung left hand, heaved up onto one knee, and fired back. The bullet was low. It struck Streeter's mount and the animal gave a piercing scream and sprang up, striking Frank's animal in the rump. It then lunged past, half turned Josh's horse, spoiling Josh's aim, and in that kaleidoscopic moment Frank saw why Bud was crying out.

Buck was down in the center of the roadway, and on across the way an injured man, supported by the express company's doorjamb, was slowly sagging earthward with a sawed-off shotgun hanging from his numbing fingers. Frank saw in a flash how that murderous charge had nearly cut Streeter in two. He fought his panicked animal away, yelling at Josh and Bud.

"Break off! Come on! Run for it!"

Bud came on, hanging in the spurs. Behind him, Josh too got clear. He was flashing east after Given when, from the bank doorway, someone opened on them with a carbine. Given twisted and fired at the same moment Josh Pendleton drew straight up in the saddle, hung there a second, then crumpled forward before falling heavily into the churned roadway. Frank had a final glimpse of Josh. He was lying out in the mud, hat gone, one leg bent grotesquely under him, firing at the bank doorway. Frank did not see who, in that doorway, was firing back.

Other weapons opened on them now as they frantically raced along. From the hotel, far back, a man was methodically firing downward and onward with some kind of a large-bore musket which made a terrifically loud and deep roar.

Frank did not twist to return the gunshots. He concentrated on getting clear. Behind him,

Bud Given had shot out his hand gun and was now firing rearward with one hand, using his Winchester carbine.

Fresh battlers kept joining this running battle. Frank was well down the roadway eastward when a wild-eyed man in red underwear and lacking both a coat and shirt, jumped out of a house upon the porch, threw up a rifle, and fired pointblank at Frank. The bullet swept away a tuft of mane hair from in front of Frank's saddle, and his horse gave a wild onward bound that spoiled this man's second shot.

Bud Given, brought around by this close firing, cried out something in a ragged voice, leveled his Winchester using both hands now and dragged off a shot.

The householder upon the porch flung his rifle away from him as though it had stung him, jumped high into the air, and fell, breaking over in the middle and coming to rest, head-down upon one side of a railing and feet-down upon the other side.

Given's mount stumbled, went down on both knees, and skidded along for some four or five feet on an icy wagon rut, then Bud fought it back upright again. For Frank, who was riding twisted when this happened, it was a bad moment. Far back, he could see townsmen pouring out into the roadway and firing wildly in their general direction. This was no time for either he or Bud to fall into the hands of that crowd.

He cried out, encouraging Bud. Given looked up, his face soiled and twisted and his eyes wide-sprung but looking vacant. Then the bad moment was past and they were rushing along again. But in that one moment Frank had seen something in Given's expression. A kind of knowledge Bud possessed. A strange certainty which meant only one thing, and this odd thought filled Frank's mind now, as though nothing else mattered, as though the world was not crashing down around him, as though he was face to face with another man's destiny and had to get away lest it touch him with its cold fingers, too.

"Frank!"

He heard as though from a great distance. He knew the voice and understood its desperation. He flung a backward look where Bud was losing steadily in his race to catch up.

"Frank! My horse . . . !"

Given's animal did not fall or crumple. He simply ran on, going lower and lower, running down into the mud until he fell heavily and up-ended and skidded along in the dirty snow, throwing his rider clear. Given skidded too, then, only he was flinging about with his arms and hands, and the Winchester was gone now. The horse had been fatally hit. He was dead.

"Frank . . . !"

Chapter Sixteen

Galloway and Clem Houston heard that far-away muffled great blast simultaneously at their table in the café. Without a word or a glance, they both sprang up. Galloway's chair went over backward with a clatter. Houston let out a cry.

"The bank!"

Galloway flung out of the café. Houston was close on his heels. They broke past the plank walk, stumbling in icy roadway slush because of that parked, big freight wagon which they otherwise could not see around. Galloway saw a man down in the mud opposite the express office, but he had heard no gunshot. He could not have, because the express company's shotgun guard had traded shots with Buck Streeter at the identical moment Frank Reno had blown up the bank's safe. He saw a man stagger to the very edge of the express company's doorway and lean there, a riot-gun dangling from his hands. Then Galloway sighted those rushing figures at the hitch rack in front of the bank. He recognized only one of them—Frank Reno. With a ripped-out curse Galloway went for his gun.

Houston, at Galloway's side but slightly farther out in the roadway, also went into action. Galloway saw the younger man draw his gun and fire up the roadway where those milling figures at the hitch rack were flinging astride. Galloway also fired, twice in rapid succession. He had caught sight of those unmistakable cloth sacks Frank Reno had around his saddle horn. He knew instinctively what they contained, and he tried hard to bring Reno down. Neither of his bullets, however, struck Reno, but they did come close enough to Josh Pendleton to bring him around under the mistaken impression that he, not Frank Reno, was under personal attack.

Galloway saw that muzzle-blasting red-orange lash of flame and it appeared to spear dead at him from Pendleton's gun. Then he heard that slug tear cloth and flesh and bone and he turned his head the slightest bit. Houston's hair tossed from the impact. He staggered backward one step, and then he wilted. Galloway saw Houston drop his gun, throw out both hands, and sink down into the mud. He had no time to see anything more than this. From up by the bank, gunfire was swelling now into a fusillade. Galloway set his legs wide and thumbed off shots. He saw one of the outlaws break out of that plunging mass of horses at the bank hitch rack and he tried for a calm shot. As he was bringing his gun to bear, however, a bullet struck him hard. He did not know who had fired the shot. He did not have time to wonder even where it had hit him. He only felt a sledge-like blow somewhere below his belt, and from instinct he flung out a hand and arm to break the fall. He did not think of pain. He had no time for that. He felt the ice and mud though, as that flung-out hand went deep into them there in the roadway and that shock of bitter cold flashed up along his nerves.

Yet he did not quite go all the way down. He hung a moment, fighting for balance, then heaved upward into a kneeling position and brought his gun up again. He fired it as the outlaws fled eastward along the roadway. Other weapons were also firing now. Somewhere close by and overhead, he heard a big Sharps rifle boom and pause and boom again.

He saw the last fleeing rider stiffen, draw upright, then tumble and sprawl in the mud. Galloway coldly aimed at this man's gun flash, held steady, and squeezed.

The big gun bucked in his fist, the sprawled man jerked and flopped and rolled over to lie still, his gun flung away, both of his arms out their full length in the dirt. Galloway fired at that inert form again and again, until his gun went empty, then he holstered it and put down both hands into the mud and pushed, and unsteadily got upright again.

Now, he could feel the pain. He had been hit in the lower muscles of the left leg. The injury ached more than it actually pained him, but above all other considerations Galloway was enraged. He did not particularly mind that Clem Houston lay dead. He scarcely considered the two other motionless figures in the ooze of that churned roadway, either—Buck Streeter and Josh Pendleton. He had his savage and piercing gaze fixed far ahead where two desperate horsemen were fleeing along in a whipping easterly flight from Brigham town. He wanted those other two men dead also. This moment, he wanted *that* more than anything else in life.

He started moving, awkwardly and unsteadily, and he reloaded his hand gun as he went, unconscious that he was bellowing for a horse until, at the livery barn's entrance, he saw the ashen, badly shaken day man run away from him deeper into the barn. Then Galloway stopped, stood with blood filling his left boot, and glared.

"Fetch me a horse, god-damn you!" he roared after the hostler. "Fetch me out a horse at once!" He said more than that—folks afterward recalled—but this was in substance the body of his repeated cry. "Hurry up with that horse, you son- . . . !"

He broke off to hear a carbine slam its solid roar up where the outlaws were racing. He saw the puff of smoke and heard another carbine answer. Then the trembling liveryman appeared with a saddled beast and Galloway, still gripping his reloaded pistol, dragged himself up and across leather, jerked the reins, fetching the animal smartly around, and he unmercifully gored him with his right spur. The horse lunged and whistled at the same time, nearly unseating Galloway. He lit down hard in a free-reined run, flinging upward great gobbets of icy mud. The liveryman stood there straining to see, one hand raised to protect his face from that flying ice-cold earth.

Galloway careened in pursuit of Frank Reno and Bud Given. He fired once and the livery animal, wise in the ways of his kind, was slowing when that shot exploded over its head. The beast instantly struck its top speed and kept onward at that furious gait. Galloway was closing the long distance. He fired again and afterward watched Given's animal run on, going slower and slower until it fell heavily and skidded, hurling its rider free. Galloway saw Given's gun fly from the outlaw's hand. He drew a bead on Given, but the luck that had allowed him one hit from the plunging back of his animal did not smile again and Galloway's third shot went wide.

Until now Galloway had not seen Frank Reno fire a single shot. Now he did. Reno, seeing Given unhorsed in the mud, hauled back, whipped his gun up, and twice fired back in the lawman's direction. Galloway felt the cold breath of those slugs. He instinctively yanked back his reins and fought the sliding horse around. He let off one shot, but with no thought of striking Reno, only deterring him. Then he pushed the livery animal toward a wide opening between two houses and ran in there for protection. His mount had an iron mouth and could not be completely checked and swung around until Galloway was on out into the rear yard of one of those houses. Then, with rolling eyes, the horse went back toward the roadway under Galloway's fierce urgings.

Quite suddenly there was silence. Galloway looked out, saw Reno's horse standing riderless and wide-legged, its sides heaving, and beyond it the corpse of Given's animal. But neither outlaw was in sight. Galloway considered this. Reno's animal still had the two tied flour sacks upon its saddle, the carbine in its boot, and the bedroll aft of the cantle. Galloway sat entirely still. He began a systematic probing with his shifting gaze for the two men who were now afoot on the outskirts of Brigham.

He did not push on out into the roadway to make of himself an easy target, but he dismounted instead, lurched, caught himself with a thrown-out left hand, and leaned upon the wooden siding of one of the houses. His left foot felt slippery in its boot.

Westerly toward the center of town, men were forming, calling out to one another, rushing without direction here and there but making a general eastward advance. Galloway thought he had only to wait now, that the crowd would do the work for him. He also thought he did not want Reno and Given to go like that—dragged behind someone's horse at the end of a lariat through the mud of the streets to where the agitated townsmen would hang them. A man's greatest enemies deserved better than that. They deserved to go out in a burst of flame and thunder. Galloway had suffered the agonies of a relentless pursuit to get where he now stood. He did not propose to see a herd of idiots interpose now with their mindless voices and their pointless excitement.

Somewhere, across the roadway among those yonder sharks, two panting outlaws in fear for their lives, were lying close and waiting for a miracle.

Galloway opened the gate of his six-gun cylinder, began to punch out spent loads and plug in fresh ones from his belt. *Miracles didn't happen anymore,* he thought; *they hadn't happened for hundreds of years and they would not happen now*. He finished with the gun, dropped it away into its holster, and leaned there, looking across the road. *End of the trail,* he thought. *End of the trail, Given and Reno. But, by God, you're men, especially you, Reno, to get down and leave your horse and that money to help Given. You're a damned sight better man than those oncoming howling townsmen are.*

It did not occur to John Galloway that the hunted and the hunter became, in their final hours, akin in more than simply thought and action, and furthermore it never had occurred to him—and if it ever had he would have vehemently denied it—that those who served the law and those who opposed it, were not so vastly different at all. Particularly in their violence were they alike.

The houses across from him were shacks, actually. Even their settings in soft snow could not entirely erase that look of poverty, of want, which permeated this end of town. One of them he recalled as being the place where he'd seen Reno and that woman talking. That one, he now thought, would be where the outlaws were lying together now, scarcely breathing, and with fear like a lead weight in their bellies.

The first hurrying townsmen were coming up. Galloway turned to see them. They had shotguns, rifles, pistols, and carbines. Their faces were contorted with excitement and they constantly cried out to one another. They came flinging along in full sight, reckless in their exuberance. *Foolishly reckless,* Galloway thought.

He pushed up off the siding and limped out to meet them. They saw him and slowed, became quieter, eddied up around him, with more approaching. He put his hostile glare upon those nearest but said nothing until at least twenty men were there. Then he jerked a thumb in the direction of Frank Reno's panting horse.

He said: "There's your money. Go get it. Take

it back to the bank. Take the horse to the livery barn."

A powerfully-built man carrying a coiled bull-whip, wearing an oversized blanket coat and bearded to the ears, asked: "Where are they? They got to be around here somewhere."

Galloway looked at this man. He said: "You stay with me. You got a pistol?"

The teamster opened his coat to reveal a holstered six-gun.

Galloway nodded, repeating what he'd said again and looking among the others for a match to the burly freighter. A dark man, better dressed than the others and with knife scars on his face, was standing there. Like the teamster this man had not drawn his belt gun, either. He was puffing a little from the running but he was quiet and his eyes were calm.

"You, too," Galloway told this man, who happened to be Dell Smith, owner of the Big Elk saloon, and with these selections he had completed his choosing.

"The rest of you go on back. I mean it. I don't want any of you up here. Take your money and go on back. Pick up those dead men in the roadway and put 'em away, and stay out of this end of town."

The crowd of men was quite silent. One or two of them recognized Galloway, like Platt the barber and the day man from the livery barn, but they had no idea who he was. Still, Galloway's look and his words commanded them. They would have gone away even if Galloway hadn't identified himself as a deputy U.S. federal marshal. After he did this, they began to murmur among themselves, to shuffle their feet and shrug and drift away.

Galloway waited, too, until they had taken the flour sacks from Reno's animal, until they were going back toward the heart of town, leading the horse and talking among themselves, scuffling along dragging their weapons and beginning to feel that drained-dry sensation that came after moments of high excitement.

Then he considered the bearded man and the knife-scarred man, his voice touching each of them in a dulled-out way, explaining to them who the outlaws were, how he had been hunting them for so long, and now what he thought, which was that they were close by, that they would not die easily, that they would never surrender to be lynched.

The knife-scarred man said calmly: "Marshal, you're hit. We better take time out to care for that."

"I'll live," replied Galloway crankily. "We won't take time out for anything until afterward." He turned, jutted his chin across the way, and said: "See that shack? Either of you know the woman who lives there?"

Dell Smith spoke up. "I know her. Mary Wilson. Her man died of lung fever couple years back. She's got a kid."

"I think that's where they'll be hiding," stated Galloway. "You got the guts to walk over there, mister, and get her an' the kid out of the house?"

Smith considered Mary Wilson's house for a time, then he said: "Yeah. The kid won't be there. He'll be at school. You two fellers cover me."

"I don't think Given and Reno'll shoot. Not unless you stumble onto them."

"You sure of that?" Dell Smith asked dryly.

Galloway swore. "Of course I'm not sure of it. If you don't want to go, I'll do it."

Now the bearded teamster spoke up, saying: "Hell, weak as you are, feller, you wouldn't get half way across the road. I'll go."

But Dell Smith contradicted the freighter. "No. You two stay here. Keep your eyes peeled and, if anything happens, be damned careful of your shots." He started forward, moved out into the roadway slush and did not once look back.

CHAPTER SEVENTEEN

Reno had no idea that Bud had been hit until he left his mount to go to Given's aid. Until he'd lifted the stunned man from the roadway mud and began to drag him onward toward his own horse, thinking they'd continue their flight riding double. Then he saw the blood, the hopeless look in Given's eyes, and he stood there supporting him, wondering what he must now do.

"Go on," said Bud. "What's the use . . . us both goin' out in this dirty little town? Go on, Frank."

It was too late for that, and Frank knew it. He threw an arm around Given and tried to hurry along southward out of the road with him. Given's legs worked well enough. They made it to the side of a house, down the side, and out to a ramshackle shed. Frank, struck by vague familiarity as they entered this frigid place, stepping deep into its moldy shadows, discovered with a start where he was—in Mary Wilson's unused old lean-to out behind the house.

He put Given down where some dry hay was, opened his coat, and saw the gelatin-like shininess of congealing blood. Given had been shot through from back to front, low in the body. He seemed not to appreciate the seriousness of his injury though, for, after examining it briefly, he looked at Frank saying: "Go on. Get out of here. They'll find us. Get clear, Frank."

Reno closed the coat and rocked back on his heels. "Too late," he said. "Too late for that now, Bud. If we lie low, they might not find us in here."

"The hell they won't," responded Given bitterly. "The whole damned town's up in arms. Frank, did they get Josh, too?"

"Yeah."

"Well . . ." Bud lapsed into silence. He drew his six-gun and let it lie in his lap. He did not appear interested in the sounds around their shed, at all. "I should've known I couldn't expect much different than this. Frank? You know how a feller thinks? Each raid would be the last one. Then I'd return to my wife and kid in Kansas. We'd buy a good farm. . . . I should've known. . . ."

Frank heard without heeding. He was listening to those oncoming howls, how they raised and joined together in their clamoring. He heard them come up close and dwindle to full silence. He strained now, wondering about that stillness. He crept to the doorless opening, lay flat, and peered out. He saw men take the sacks from his saddle, heft them, then lead his mount along westward with them. He began desperately to hope this would be enough. When that mob had trudged beyond sight, he saw three men across the road, talking. One he recognized as that tall man with the droopy mustache who had single-handedly pursued them. Another he recognized as the owner of the saloon back in town. The third man had his back to Frank. He did not know this one.

He watched them talking together. He saw the man from the saloon start out across the road toward the Wilson house. He watched this man go along the side of the house, pause and raise his fist to knuckle the door, then step back one pace and put his searching eyes out over the yard, the shed, the house. Then the door opened.

Frank could not hear the saloon man speak. Neither could he see Mary Wilson until, a moment later, she stepped down into the yard, put her shawl about her shoulders, and strode away with the saloon man. Frank watched them walk away. He knew why this was. He wriggled clear, got to one knee, and struck chaff from his clothing. Then he crossed over to Bud to say: "They know we're in here. They just took the woman out of the house. They'll surround the place next, Bud. Bud . . . ?"

Bud Given was dead with his head wearily low and the six-gun lying quiet in his lap.

Frank was the last of the Streeters. He was alone with the only one of those outlaws he had ever really cared for—dead Bud Given. And now he was waiting for what was inevitable.

As sometimes happens during quiet moments such as this, memories came. He had a terrible

189

longing to be what he had once been, and his mistakes gave him cruel pain. He despised himself for what he had allowed himself to become. He despised Buck, too, and Josh Pendleton, and, as this moment passed with its strong silence, its hopelessness, he felt inexpressibly lonely.

One by one, Frank knew each of the times in his life when he had made his mistakes, when he had turned the wrong way. They rose up before him now with terrible clarity and the excuses he had sold himself on then, in each case, was now there to mock him with falseness. He thought of Mary Wilson's handsomeness, of her warmth, and of her smile. He also thought of her son, but no softening touched his features for these recollections. Nothing at all changed the tired, ill, and disillusioned mask of his face.

"Hey, Reno! Frank Reno! Give up! Throw out your gun and give up!"

Frank did not know that voice but he had no trouble placing it. The caller was around front of Mary Wilson's house. He sank down beside Given on both his knees and dully punched out the spent casings from his six-gun and punched in loaded ones. The next call came from behind the shed.

"Come out, Reno! Don't be a damned fool. You don't have a prayer of a chance left."

This voice, though hard and bitter and

unrelenting, sounded less excited than the other one. It called forth again.

"Frank, this is U.S. Marshal John Galloway. I promise you there'll be no lynching. Now come out of there."

There would be no lynching. Frank agreed with this as he twisted, looking for a bulwark to get behind. There was none, only a rotting old manger. There would be no lynching at all for the simple reason that they would not get him.

"Reno! This is your last chance!" cried that second voice, sounding stern now. "Don't be a damned fool. You can't get clear and your friends are gone. Listen to me, Reno. I don't know whether you've ever heard of John Galloway or not, but I can tell you two things. I've never gone back on my word and I've never failed to bring in my man. I give you my word you'll not be molested by these people. I also give you my word I'll bring you in. Now come out of there."

Frank put out a hand to topple Given. He laid him out flat, clear of harm's way, then he squirmed forward, went flat by the doorway, poked out his pistol, cocked it, and fired it. There was no target. He wasn't seeking one.

Instantly three guns blazed back. Dust flew, slivers broke off the rotting manger, and one lead slug shivered the wall a foot over Frank's head.

He fired again, this time toward the front of the house where he'd seen a blur of movement. His slug tore away a piece of wood siding. He felt badly about that. It was a tired little house and there was no money in it to repair that broken board. He lowered the gun, bracing for that slashing flow of return fire.

It came again. Blind firing by men whose slitted eyes were feeling for him through rotten old wood walls. His mind was very clear now, very sharp; he heard each gunfire report with magnified importance. Bullets continued to flail the old shed, some higher up, as though seeking a man standing upright, and others slashing along low, for a kneeling or prone man.

"Reno, you fool!" roared that southward voice again. "Cut it out!"

He did not permit those men to stop their firing now. When the explosions began to atrophy, he twisted around and fired out through the rear of the shed, twice, and brought on the desired fusillade again. He did not wish to hear that U.S. marshal's voice. He did not permit himself to think that he could, by simply walking out unarmed, stop this thing. He had a reason for this. He had been a free man all his life. Now, at the end of it, he wished to remain a free man for these last moments.

He squirmed to reload, then lay there like a man exhausted beyond hope. His mind had lost its sharpness. His nerve too was going.

"Maybe I ought to get up and run out of here,"

he said aloud to himself. "Run where?" He pushed the gun forward again, cocked it, and let it lie unfired.

Out of the yonder cold day with its light softening away toward dusk came the bullet. It struck him hard and made him gasp down deep and flex his fingers so that the cocked pistol fell into the dirt. It sent a rush of quick redness up to blur his vision, but it did not impair his voice and he cried out.

"That's all! That's all, boys, you've hit me!"

He put his head down upon one forearm feeling blissfully tired and warm all over. He heard them coming quietly, very carefully, as though they suspected a ruse. He heard one man in particular walking along unsteadily as though his legs barely braced him upright. This man paced on around the shed, and when he could see Frank's tumbled hair and hatless head low upon his arm, this man said roughly: "Never mind you two. Point your guns away. I know this one. Just stand back away."

Frank was curious about this man. He rolled his face and glanced upward. The limping man stopped, put up his gun, and awkwardly let himself down.

He said: "Are you hard hit, Frank?"

Reno said in a husky tone: "Hard hit, feller. Who are you? I don't recognize you."

"John Galloway. No. You don't know me. I

know you, though. I been trailing the lot of you a long, long time. Frank? It's got nothing to do with this . . . but tell me . . . why did you keep your secret from Buck?"

Frank tried hard to see Galloway's face better. He felt a darkness closing in on him in the shed. "How did you know about that?"

"I made it my affair to know all I could about your band, Frank. But that . . . well . . . I stumbled onto that down in Texas." Galloway put out a hand, took up Frank's gun, and uncocked it. When Frank didn't answer, Galloway said: "Hell, that's all right. I don't have to know. Just curious was all."

Frank looked upward, his head wobbled, and Galloway pushed out a supporting strong arm.

"He was my brother," said Frank. "The trouble was, after my own pa died, he was born to my ma by another man. I knew that and my ma knew it . . . but Buck never did."

"Is that why you stayed with him, Frank?"

"I guess so. Buck was all the family I had left after the war."

Galloway changed the subject. "Frank, that woman is out there. She's pretty upset . . . crying. Would you like to see her alone?"

"I'd like that," Frank murmured, and put his dimming eyes upon Galloway. "I'm obliged to you, Marshal."

Galloway muttered—"Sure."—and got up to

find the woman. "Miz Wilson?" he called out. "Hurry."

Mary Wilson came up and Galloway walked away, saying in a low growl to the teamster and the saloon man: "Get away. Go on back an' leave 'em be."

Mary knelt and held Frank, and her lips, softly pliable, changed a little, pressed together to support one another. A shadow rushed across her face when she saw that he was hard hit. She smoothed away his hair, saying: "It's all right. It's all right, Frank."

He smiled upward. "I've got lung fever anyway, ma'am. If the end hadn't come here, it'd have come soon anyway, some place else."

"I know. I knew you had the fever. You see, my husband also died of it. I know the signs, Frank."

Her eyes held a glowing deepness, a strong sweetness which made her face younger, prettier, in his fading sight. "I could give you a lot of money, ma'am. But they'd only take it away from you."

"I don't need it."

"For Don . . ."

"No, Frank. Your memory will be more to him than your money."

"Pretty . . . short memory, ma'am."

She smiled a little with her swimming eyes. "I'll not let him forget."

"And you, ma'am?"

"I'll not forget, either," she breathed. "I'll always remember how it could have ended . . . in another way, Frank. It will be something to cherish. Do you understand me?"

His gaze was a cloudy, puzzled blue. "Yes," he said, but he seemed not to see her any longer. He ran his tongue across his lips and feebly rolled his head in her lap, and faintly framed unuttered words upon his lips, then he loosened and sighed and she felt all tightness leave him, down the full length of his body. He was smiling and appeared sleepy. There was no life in him.

She did not cry at all. She looked upward after a long time and called in a voice as thin and high as a young girl's voice, which was the only indication of her anguish, and said: "Marshal, you can come back now." Then she gently placed his head upon the wintry earth and got upright to move off as Galloway limped up, his face haggard, his lips blue from blood loss, and his bitter eyes showing no triumph at all.

A high wind swept in from the mountain peaks to brush with a haunted sound over roof tops, then hasten southward. Lamps were beginning to be lighted in the heart of town. It was not really late in the day, but the clouds were billowing again. There would be another storm.

ABOUT THE AUTHOR

Lauran Paine who, under his own name and various pseudonyms has written over a thousand books, was born in Duluth, Minnesota. His family moved to California when he was at a young age and his apprenticeship as a Western writer came about through the years he spent in the livestock trade, rodeos, and even motion pictures where he served as an extra because of his expert horsemanship in several films starring movie cowboy Johnny Mack Brown. In the late 1930s, Paine trapped wild horses in northern Arizona and even, for a time, worked as a professional farrier. Paine came to know the Old West through the eyes of many who had been born in the 19th Century, and he learned that Western life had been very different from the way it was portrayed on the screen. "I knew men who had killed other men," he later recalled. "But they were the exceptions. Prior to and during the Depression, people were just too busy eking out an existence to indulge in Saturday-night brawls." He served in the U.S. Navy in the Second World War and began writing for Western pulp magazines following his discharge. It is interesting to note that his earliest novels (written under his own name and the pseudonym Mark

Carrel) were published in the British market and he soon had as strong a following in that country as in the United States. Paine's Western fiction is characterized by strong plots, authenticity, an apparently effortless ability to construct situation and character, and a preference for building his stories upon a solid foundation of historical fact. *Adobe Empire* (1956), one of his best novels, is a fictionalized account of the last twenty years in the life of trader William Bent and, in an off-trail way, has a melancholy, bittersweet texture that is not easily forgotten. In later novels like *The White Bird* (1997) and *Cache Cañon* (1998), he showed that the special magic and power of his stories and characters had only matured along with his basic themes of changing times, changing attitudes, learning from experience, respecting Nature, and the yearning for a simpler, more moderate way of life.

Books are
produced in the
United States
using U.S.-based
materials

Books are printed
using a revolutionary
new process called
THINKtech™ that
lowers energy usage
by 70% and increases
overall quality

Books are
durable and
flexible
because of
smythe-sewing

Paper is
sourced using
environmentally
responsible
foresting methods
and the
paper is acid-free

Center Point Large Print
600 Brooks Road / PO Box 1
Thorndike, ME 04986-0001 USA

(207) 568-3717

US & Canada:
1 800 929-9108
www.centerpointlargeprint.com

SPIRIT ANIMALS

SPECIAL EDITIONS

Discover the Hidden Tales of Erdas!

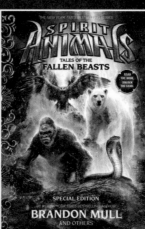

There's more to explore in the Spirit Animals world! These Special Editions reveal the secrets of Erdas in ways you never saw coming...

31901059702482

scholastic.com/spiritanimals

BOOK FOUR:

The Wyrm has awakened.

It has corrupted friends and stolen spirit animals.
It has toppled cities and poisoned the Evertree itself.

Working with the Redcloaks, the young heroes
learn of a plan to destroy this evil forever.
But they'll only get one chance. And if they fail,
the world will be consumed.

scholastic.com/spiritanimals